Ronni glanced over at Cole on her way out the door, only to find that he was leaning back in his chair, watching her as she suspected.

He smiled again, and her heart did a funny little jump in her chest. She sloshed her coffee a bit and was glad it had a lid to catch the warm liquid. She felt she had to say something before walking out the door. "You two have a good day."

"You, too," Cole said as he got up and opened the door for her.

She did have her hands full with the sandwich that was getting cold, the coffee cup, and her purse, and she appreciated his help. "Thank you."

He looked into her eyes and inclined his head. "You are welcome."

The breath caught in Ronni's throat, and it wasn't until the door shut behind her that she could let it out. He was one nice-looking man. His hair was light brown, and his eyes were the color of cinnamon. She was spending *way* too much time thinking about Cole Bannister, she told herself as she got in the car and started it up. Hadn't she decided never to let herself become interested in anyone again? And wasn't she determined that she'd not let her happiness or her livelihood depend on another man. . .ever again?

"Yes!" Ronni answered her thoughts out loud.

Besides, his visit had nothing to do with her and everything to do with Claudia, she told herself. She really knew nothing about him, but his consideration of Claudia and the obvious love they felt for one another had gone a long way in convincing Ronni that his visit would be good for her mother-in-law. . .if uncomfortable for her. She'd just try to avoid being around him as much as she could while he was here.

JANET LEE BARTON and her husband, Dan, reside in southern Mississippi and feel blessed to have at least one daughter and her family living nearby. Janet loves being able to share her faith and love of the Lord through her writing. She's very happy that the kind of romances the Lord has called her to write can be read by and shared with women of all ages.

Books by Janet Lee Barton

HEARTSONG PRESENTS
HP434—Family Circle
HP532—A Promise Made
HP562—Family Ties
HP623—A Place Called Home
HP644—Making Amends
HP689—Unforgettable

To
Love Again

Janet Lee Barton

Heartsong Presents

To my Lord and Savior for showing me the way.

And, to all of those living along the Gulf Coast—from Florida to Texas—and especially to the State of Mississippi. When hurricanes come our way, I pray that the Lord will give us the wisdom to know when to evacuate, the courage to come back in, the comfort only He can give for the losses we might suffer, and the determination to rebuild and make our communities ones that seek His will and guidance always.

A note from the Author:
I love to hear from my readers! You may correspond with me by writing:

Janet Lee Barton
Author Relations
PO Box 721
Uhrichsville, OH 44683

ISBN 1-59789-087-1

TO LOVE AGAIN

Scripture taken from the HOLY BIBLE, NEW INTERNATIONAL VERSION®. NIV®. Copyright © 1973, 1978, 1984 by International Bible Society. Used by permission of Zondervan. All rights reserved.

All of the characters and events in this book are fictitious. Any resemblance to actual persons, living or dead, or to actual events is purely coincidental.

Our mission is to publish and distribute inspirational products offering exceptional value and biblical encouragement to the masses.

PRINTED IN THE U.S.A.

one

Cole Bannister was on his way out the door when the shrill ring of the telephone stopped him in his tracks. He had a mind to let the answering machine pick up, but it was unusual for him to get a call at home this early in the day. He shook his head and turned back into the house. Striding across polished wooden floors to the telephone alcove in the foyer, he picked up the receiver on the fourth ring.

Probably a wrong number, Cole thought as he spoke. "Hello."

"Cole? Is that you?"

"Yes, Aunt Claudia, it's me." His aunt's voice had sounded a little flustered, so he quickly added, "I'm here. Is something wrong?"

"I think there is. . .and I believe I might need your help in trying to figure out just how bad things are."

"What do you mean 'how bad things are'?" Cole sat down in the chair next to the telephone table. "What is wrong?"

"Oh, Cole. . .I think I may have to sell the house to pay off some of the debt Brian left me in."

"How could Brian have left *you* in debt, Aunt Claudia?"

"I don't know, Cole. I just know that all of a sudden I have people calling and demanding payment on debts I'm sure I never made. And I'm having trouble balancing my bank account."

Cole ran a hand over his brow as he wondered if his

aunt was all right. She certainly didn't sound like the strong woman he'd always known her to be, and she wasn't making any sense.

"Cole, are you still there? Can you come help me out?"

"Yes, I'm here. And of course I can, Aunt Claudia. I'll be there tomorrow evening." He had a meeting he would have to put off, but Aunt Claudia had been like a mother to him after his own mother died. She'd never asked anything in return—until now. Rescheduling an appointment was the least he could do.

"Thank you, dear. I know it's probably an imposition for you, but—"

Cole hurried to reassure her. "Aunt Claudia, it is past time I took a few days off and paid you a visit. I'll be there in time for supper tomorrow evening, okay?"

"More than okay." Cole could hear the relief in her voice as she added, "Come hungry."

Cole chuckled. His aunt loved to feed people. "I will. See you tomorrow, Aunt Claudia."

"See you then, dear," his aunt said before she hung up.

Cole made a mental list of all the things he needed to do before taking off. He'd have his secretary cancel any appointments he had over the next few days, book his flight out of Dallas, and make arrangements to have a rental car ready when he arrived in Gulfport. He'd drive over to Magnolia Bay from there.

As he drove to the offices of his company, Bannister Designs, he told himself not to worry. But something had to be wrong if Aunt Claudia thought she was broke. Why, the Melrose family was one of the wealthiest in South Mississippi. He knew she'd been left well off by his uncle t didn't happen that way.

ow, Ronni finally felt as if she was living again. . .
ing forward instead of backward. "Thank You, Lord,"
whispered as she turned up the road to Melrose
anor.

Huge live oaks lined the drive, their limbs draped with
ray-green moss. Ronni still felt like somewhat of an
nterloper living in this grand old home. In the late eighteen
hundreds, the Melrose family, who lived in New Orleans
at the time, built the manor as a summer home. Over
the years, the Melroses had moved from Louisiana and
eventually made Magnolia Bay the family home, becoming
some of the town's leading citizens.

Ronni pulled her car around the circle drive to the back
of the house and noticed that Claudia's vehicle was gone.
Then she remembered that Claudia had mentioned that
morning something about a city council meeting she had
to attend. Letting herself in the house, Ronni checked the
note board by the back door to see if Claudia had left her
any instructions for starting dinner. No note. Ronni sighed
and headed toward the back staircase in the kitchen. She'd
go change and then come back down and see what she
could come up with to make a light supper.

No matter how many times Ronni climbed the staircases
in this house, she was sure she would always marvel that
she was living in such a beautiful place. She loved her room.
Claudia had told her to decorate it any way she wanted, but
Ronni liked it just fine as it was.

Soft yellow walls and carpet were the perfect backdrop
r the aqua, yellow, and green floral drapes and bed linens,
d her private bathroom was done mostly in aqua with

Drew. And he didn't think there was any way Brian could
have gotten into her funds. Besides, Brian had been dead
for nearly a year.

Cole shook his head. Something was wrong. He pulled
into his parking lot, got out of the car, and sprinted to his
office. He was anxious to get to Magnolia Bay and find out
what it was.

❧

"Think it would be okay if I took off a few minutes
early?" Ronni Melrose asked her best friend and employer,
Meagan Chambers.

"Sure. Laura will be in any minute. Nothing is wrong, is
there?"

Ronni shook her head and smiled. "No. I think I just
have a case of spring fever."

"Well that's good to hear." Meagan chuckled. "It is a
lovely day."

She followed Ronni back to the small kitchen where
she'd gone to get her purse. "How is Claudia doing these
days?"

"Pretty good. She's seemed a little preoccupied lately—
not quite like herself." Claudia Melrose had been such a
rock during the last year, but lately she seemed quieter than
usual and even a little worried. But when Ronni had asked
Claudia about it, the older woman had assured her nothing
was wrong. "I hope she's not coming down with anything."

"I hope not, too. You have a nice evening and tell
Claudia hello for me," Meagan said.

"I will, Meagan. You and Nick have a good evening, too.
I'll see you in the morning."

Ronni headed down the steps and out to the parking

lot. She loved her work as assistant manager of Meagan's Color Cottage, and she was very thankful for it. But today she was glad to be going home. It had been a beautiful February day, and she'd fought the urge to be outside all afternoon. She suddenly wanted to plant anything that would bloom in the next few weeks. Maybe she had early spring fever. . .or something. Whatever it was, Ronni welcomed the feeling.

She got in her car and pulled onto Bay Drive, Magnolia Bay's main street that ran parallel to the bay. The water glistened in the late afternoon sun, and Ronni reveled in the sudden realization that she felt at peace, as if all were right with the world.

Nearly a year after becoming a widow, she was beginning to think that she might finally be getting over the broken dream of what her marriage could have been—and recovering from the death of her husband.

The last year had been a nightmare. No. It had been more than a year. It seemed she and Brian had only been together a short time before they started having problems. Looking back, Ronni could almost pinpoint when their trouble began.

Brian enjoyed living on the Mississippi Gulf Coast, and he loved the nightlife the casinos in the area provided. At first she'd gone with him; she hadn't been a Christian when they met and fell in love. But after they became engaged and she began attending church with Brian and his mother—as he said was expected of them—she didn't feel quite right about going to the casinos. She hadn't been raised to go to church, and she'd been surprised at how much she enjoyed being there.

After they were married, Brian didn't [...] getting up on Sunday mornings and going [...] she went without him, sitting beside Claudi[...] up everything she could from God's Word. A[...] passed, it didn't take Ronni long to fall in lo[...] Lord and become a Christian herself.

That was when the problems between her an[...] really started. But she didn't want to think about[...] that now. She wanted to be thankful for her bles[...] Ronni stopped at a red traffic light and expelled a [...] breath. Without the Lord, she truly didn't know w[...] she would have done. He had been there, taking care [...] the details and seeing to it that all of her needs were met[...] When her mother-in-law found out Brian had gambled[...] all their money away, nothing would do for Claudia but to have Ronni move into Melrose Manor with her. At first Ronni was reluctant, but then she recognized the pain in Claudia's eyes. Not only had the older woman lost her only son, but like Ronni, she'd had to face the fact that he was[...] the man she thought he was. Ronni had finally agreed[...] move in with her, unable to bear leaving Claudia— woman who'd brought her to the Lord—all alone.

She and Claudia had clung to their faith and to[...] other, and the Lord had comforted them as only He [...] Thanks to Him, to her mother-in-law, and to the f[...] she'd made in Magnolia Bay, Ronni was beginn[...] realize that she was not to blame for Brian's weakn[...] for his drifting away from the Lord. He'd done t[...] before she met him. She wished with all her heart[...] turned back to the Lord. . .that they could have[...] one in their marriage and their faith, but it wasn'[...]

touches of yellow. There was a comfortable sitting area in front of a working fireplace and a balcony that looked out onto the back garden, where the pink and white azaleas would be in bloom in a few weeks.

After changing into jeans and a soft green top, Ronni took her hair out of the chignon she'd worn to work and brushed it free, fluffing the curly auburn mass around her face and letting it tumble down her back. She hurried back downstairs and entered the modern, updated kitchen just as Claudia walked in the back door.

Ronni rushed to relieve her of the heavy bags she was carrying.

"Thank you, dear. There are a few more sacks in the car."

"I'll bring them in," Ronni said. "I didn't realize you were going grocery shopping, too."

There were quite a few more bags, and Ronni wondered why Claudia had bought so much. But she seemed happy, and if stocking the pantry could put that lilt in her voice, then it was all fine with Ronni.

"I'm glad you didn't start anything for dinner," Claudia said as Ronni brought in the last few bags and began putting things up. "I picked up a roasted chicken and some potato salad at the grocery store. . .and a cheesecake for dessert. The meeting lasted a little longer than I thought it would."

"Roast chicken sounds wonderful to me. I wish it was warm enough for us to eat outside," Ronni said as the older woman took the chicken out of the bag and opened the plastic container it came in. "Do you want to eat in here or in the dining room?"

"Let's eat here at the breakfast table," Claudia said. "It will be dark soon, but we can look outside even if it is still too cool to eat out there. In another month, we'll be able to."

"I know. I love March down here." Ronni set the table with place mats and silverware as Claudia fixed their plates and brought them over.

They bowed their heads, and when Claudia finished saying the blessing, she looked over at Ronni and smiled. "It was a beautiful day today, wasn't it?"

"Oh yes, it was." Ronni chuckled. "I found myself wanting to dig a hole and plant something. . .anything."

Claudia laughed. "I'm thrilled to hear you say that, dear. We'll have to make a trip to the nursery and get you some bulbs to plant."

Ronni was pleased to see that her mother-in-law looked much better than she had at breakfast that morning. Her blue eyes had their normal sparkle, and Ronni breathed a little sigh of relief that Claudia seemed herself again. "How was the meeting? I hope it was productive."

"Well, I think so. We're going to begin taking applications for a city manager and look into getting a publicity person to help us sell Magnolia Bay as a wonderful family place to vacation and live."

"That sounds like a good plan to me. I'm sure there are a lot of people who would like to have a family-friendly place to stay where they could be close to the beaches."

"I'll always wish the casinos had never come to the coast of Mississippi," Claudia said. "But they did, and they are a fact of life we have to live with. I am just so proud that Magnolia Bay had the moral courage to say no when the casinos tried to locate in our town—even though it cost the town revenue and. . .a lot more." Claudia sighed deeply and shook her head. "In the end, it didn't keep Brian from going to them. . . ."

Ronni reached across the table and patted her mother-in-law's hand. "No, but it didn't make it easier for him, either, Claudia."

The older woman patted her back, seeming to pull herself together once more. "You are right, dear. And thankfully, the rest of the city council is as determined as I am to bring Magnolia Bay back to life."

"I'm sure it will grow again. After all, the Lord is on our side."

Claudia smiled and nodded. "Yes, He is. We just have to remember that things happen in His time, not necessarily on the timetable we'd like."

"Would you like a piece of that cheesecake now?" Ronni gathered their plates and took them over to the sink.

"Yes, but let me make some coffee to go with it. I have some news to tell you."

"Oh? What is it?"

"I talked to my nephew, Cole, today."

Ronni had only met Cole a time or two and had never really gotten to know him, but she was aware that he was special to Claudia. "How is he?"

"Fine, I think." Claudia turned from putting on the coffee and grinned at her. "We'll know for sure soon. He's coming for a visit tomorrow!"

two

"He's coming tomorrow?" Ronni asked. *So that's why all the groceries—and the good mood.*

"Yes, Cole will be here in time for dinner," Claudia answered. "I'm so looking forward to seeing him. I need to get a room ready for him and make a pie. He loves my cooking."

"I'll get the room ready while you make a pie. Which room do you want him in?"

"The one across from Brian's old room will be fine. It's where Cole stayed when he came for visits as a boy, and he'll be comfortable there. I think I'll make an apple. If he's here long enough, I might make a peach pie, too. We have plenty in the freezer."

They had more than enough peaches in the freezer. . . and blueberries and even strawberries. Claudia hadn't quite adjusted to the fact that there was no man around to make a dent in the pies and cakes she loved to bake. Ronni hoped Cole had a big appetite. It would make her mother-in-law feel so good to feed a man again.

Claudia began planning the next night's menu while Ronni cleared the table and loaded the dishwasher.

"Cole always loved my fried chicken and mashed potatoes. I think I'll make that for tomorrow night. Poor dear, being single, I'm sure he doesn't get much home cooking."

"Probably not. I'm sure he'll love anything you want to make, Mom." It was easy to call Claudia by that name. Ronni's own mother had passed away when she was in college, and Brian's mom had treated her like a daughter from the moment they met.

"I'm just trying to remember some of his favorites. I'm so looking forward to seeing him!"

"I'll go get the room ready and be back in a little while and help peel those apples for you."

"Thank you, dear." Claudia looked up from her recipe binder and smiled at Ronni. "Have I told you lately how much I love you and how glad I am that you moved in with me?"

Ronni chuckled. "Yes, you have. Daily. I've never felt more at home anywhere than I do here, Mom. And I love you, too."

Claudia nodded. "I know you do."

Ronni left her to her recipes and headed upstairs to prepare Cole's room. She was glad Claudia hadn't given him Brian's old bedroom. She didn't like to go in there. It was a teenager's room, and from the mementos her mother-in-law clung to, Ronni couldn't recognize the man she'd been married to.

The room Cole would be using had been redecorated a few years back, and Ronni was sure he would be comfortable there. Done in blue and cream, it was large and comfortable. It, too, had a sitting area in front of a fireplace and a balcony that looked out onto one of the huge magnolias surrounding the house.

Ronni put fresh linens on the bed and fluffed the pillows. She dusted and gave the room a good vacuuming. The once-a-month cleaning lady wasn't due to come in until next week, and Claudia would feel better knowing the room had been cleaned.

Taking one last look around the room, Ronni wished the cleaning was all it would take for her to feel better. She wasn't sure why she felt so apprehensive about Cole's visit, but she did. Maybe it was simply because she didn't know this cousin of Brian's all that well—and wasn't sure she wanted to. Or it could be that Claudia hadn't said who had initiated the idea of a stay, and Ronni couldn't help but be curious as to why Cole was suddenly coming to Mississippi. She tried to shake off her uneasiness about it all as she flipped off the light switch.

By the time she returned downstairs, Claudia had her piecrusts made and most of the apples peeled. She waived Ronni's offer to help aside. "Just pour a cup of coffee and keep me company."

Ronni did just that, praying that the lift in Claudia's mood lasted. Aware that it was due to Cole's visit, Ronni asked the Lord to help her try to make their guest welcome, too.

❧

By the time she left for work the next morning, Ronni felt calmer about Cole's visit. Claudia was so excited; she'd changed the menu several times before handing Ronni a list of grocery items she'd forgotten the day before.

It didn't matter how she felt about Brian's cousin coming for a visit, Ronni told herself. What truly mattered was seeing the sparkle back in Claudia's eyes. That alone was enough to start Ronni's day off right. As she drove downtown, her spring fever mood from the day before returned, and she made a mental note to pick up a gardening magazine when she went to the grocery store.

"Good morning," she called as she entered the shop.

"Good morning, Ronni! Isn't it a beautiful day?" Meagan asked, looking up from the cash register where she was putting the day's starting cash. She almost glowed with happiness these days.

Ronni chuckled and agreed. "It is. But then, every day has been beautiful to you since you and Nick got married."

Meagan laughed. "That's very true. I love being married to Nick."

"Well, the two of you deserve to be happy. You certainly waited long enough to get together." Meagan and Nick had been high school sweethearts who'd broken up with each other and gone separate ways until last year when Meagan came back to Magnolia Bay to open her second shop. It had been rocky at first, but finally, they'd come to the realization that they were meant to be together.

"And now I feel that each day together is a blessing from the Lord," Meagan said. "He does have a plan for each of us; I am certain of that."

Ronni nodded. She felt that was true, too. But she wasn't expecting to have the kind of happiness Meagan was enjoying now. She didn't think she'd ever be willing to risk having her heart broken again. . .or that there was any man out there she could trust enough to take the risk.

"Oh, Ronni, I'm sorry. I am so thoughtless at times."

"Meagan, what are you talking about?"

"I shouldn't be going on and on about how happy I am when you are still dealing with losing your husband."

"There is absolutely no reason why you shouldn't be

vocal about your joy, Meagan. I know you wish things were different for me, but it's okay. I'm all right. More than all right, actually. I'm feeling alive again and looking forward to each day. That's a blessing."

"Oh, I'm glad to hear that. I pray that you will find someone—"

"I don't think that's in the Lord's plans for me. . .and that's fine, too."

"But—"

Ronni held up a hand and interrupted her friend once more. "That doesn't mean the Lord doesn't have a plan for me, Meagan. I just don't think it involves falling in love again. And unless He lets me know differently, I'll take my cue from the book of Ruth and be here for Claudia."

"Kind of like Naomi and Ruth?"

Ronni nodded. "Yes, kind of like that."

Meagan had a thoughtful look in her eyes. Then she grinned and said, "Hmm. . .you do remember that—"

"Hello! Are you open yet?" Mrs. Myers asked, peeking around the door and effectively putting an end to Meagan's comment as she glanced at her watch.

"Good morning, Mrs. Myers," Meagan answered. "Yes, we are open, and you are right on time for your consultation. I'll be right with you." She handed the cash she still held in her hand to Ronni. "Will you finish this, please?"

"I'll be glad to." Still curious as to what Meagan was going to say, yet at the same time a little relieved not to hear it, Ronni took the money from her.

❧

Driving in a rented car from the Gulfport airport, Cole took the scenic route to Magnolia Bay, noticing the changes that had taken place in the last few years. He passed at least three brightly painted casinos on the coast, and attached to them were luxury hotels. Several local restaurants he remembered had given way to national chain eateries. There seemed to be more swimsuit and souvenir shops than he remembered, too. Interspersed between all of that was the charm that held because of the beautiful older homes that had been built years before. Those houses said *home* to him. . . not the casinos or new condominiums that had sprung up.

He'd almost forgotten how very much he loved spending summers in Magnolia Bay. When he turned down Bay Drive, he felt a nostalgic tug at his heart. Some things had stayed the same here, but many others had changed. The town seemed to be making some progress in trying to draw new commerce. There was Meagan's Color Cottage, owned by a friend and former resident of Dallas, and a new restaurant called the Seaside Surf and Turf. A coffee shop occupied what used to be his favorite ice cream shop, and the small movie theater seemed to be up and running. Things had changed; there was no doubt about it.

When Cole turned onto the tree-lined lane leading to the spacious old home his uncle had dubbed Melrose Manor, memories of past visits had him anticipating coming home again.

The house had all kinds of nooks and crannies for young boys to explore, and he and his cousin, Brian, had done just that. Although never close, they managed to get along when they were children, but all that changed when they became teens. Cole never understood quite why, but it seemed Brian was jealous of him. While Brian had never been a favorite of his, Cole dearly loved his aunt and uncle, so he tried to overlook their son's behavior—but it didn't always work. And by the time they became adults, Brian's attitude was increasingly hard to take, and Cole's visits had become fewer and farther between.

He sent up a prayer asking for forgiveness that he wouldn't be missing his cousin on this visit. His heart did break for his aunt, knowing that Brian's death had taken a toll on her. He was determined to do all he could to help her now. Cole pulled around to the back of Melrose Manor, feeling like a kid again, excited about coming back to the house that had been a true home to him when he'd needed one most. For a few minutes, he just sat in his car, enjoying the welcoming glow from the light in the kitchen window.

three

Ronni took off an hour early so she could get to the grocery store and be home in time to help Claudia prepare supper. When she'd talked to her earlier in the afternoon, Ronni could tell her mother-in-law seemed more than just excited. She sounded a little anxious, having second thoughts about her menu for that evening.

"I'm sure Cole will be thrilled to have your fried chicken and mashed potatoes, Mom. And no one around here makes apple pies like you do. He's going to love it all."

Claudia had sighed over the phone. "Thank you, dear. I just want him to feel like he's coming home again, and I remembered he loved my pot roast, too."

"You can do that another night. He is staying more than one, isn't he?" Not that Ronni wanted him to, but she was sure that her mother-in-law did.

"Oh yes, he is." Claudia had chuckled. "I'll have plenty of time to make his favorites."

Now as she helped Claudia with the meal, Ronni suddenly wanted to know a little more about the man who would be their houseguest. . .for no telling how long. "I don't remember much about Cole," she said as she finished adding cherry tomatoes to the salad. "What is he like?"

"He's a wonderful man. . .and was always such a sweet little boy. My brother did a good job of raising him after his wife died; but he never remarried, and I became the mother figure in Cole's life. Brian was always a little jealous of that, I think. I tried to explain that he was the lucky one, with two parents, but. . ." Claudia paused before continuing. "I think we spoiled Brian more than we thought."

Ronni had nothing to say to that. She'd tried very hard not to tell Claudia how bad things had been with her and Brian, although she suspected that her mother-in-law knew. But how could she tell the woman who'd led her to Christ that her very son wanted no part of the Savior? Or that from the moment Ronni was baptized, things between her and Brian had gone from bad to worse—until the night he'd wrapped his car around a light pole and died on the way to the hospital? Ronni fought down the memories and quickly changed the subject. "Which table should I set? The one in the dining room or the one in here?"

"Let's eat in here tonight. There's just the three of us, and I think it will make Cole feel more at home."

Ronni put fresh place mats on the table and added the place settings, glancing at the clock from time to time. It was nearly seven, and she hoped that Cole showed up before Claudia started worrying about him.

He'd come to her and Brian's wedding, and she'd seen him once or twice when he'd come for a visit with Claudia. She did remember that although Brian had never talked very much about his cousin what he had said was never very favorable. Now that she knew Brian had been jealous of him and that could have colored his comments, Ronni decided she would withhold any preconceived ideas of what Cole was like until after she really got to know him.

She heard the crunch of tires on the back drive and

looked up to see a car coming to a stop just outside. "I think he's here, Mom."

Claudia turned from checking on the chicken she'd put in the warmer and hurried to the back door. "It is him!" She rushed out to meet Cole before he even got out of the car.

Ronni watched through the window. From the hug the two shared, she could tell that this man had a very special place in Claudia's heart and her own seemed to soften somewhat. He couldn't be anywhere near what Brian had described if he could put a smile like that on Claudia's face.

❧

Cole hugged his aunt, pleased that she didn't seem as disoriented and flustered as she had on the phone. This was the Aunt Claudia he remembered.

"I am so glad you could come, dear! Let's get your bag in, and Ronni can show you to your room while I finish up supper."

Cole grabbed his suitcase and a hanging garment bag from the backseat of the car.

"One thing," aunt Claudia said as he closed the door. "I don't want Ronni to know that you came at my request. She doesn't know about this latest problem Brian left us with. She's had enough heartache. I don't want to add to it if I don't have to."

"I'll be sure and not mention your worries, then," Cole assured her as they headed for the kitchen door. "And hopefully, there's nothing to them, and she'll never have to know."

He couldn't help but wonder if Brian's wife knew more than Aunt Claudia suspected, but only time would tell. He'd find out what the trouble was. And while he was at it, he was going to enjoy being back at Melrose Manor and Magnolia Bay.

The smells that wafted out to greet him when his aunt opened the kitchen door had his mouth watering before he crossed the threshold. "Mmm, your fried chicken. I was hoping that would be what you picked."

"You always have been easy to please. I should have remembered that instead of changing my mind ten times since yesterday." His aunt chuckled, and he followed her inside.

The kitchen was much as he remembered it except for the woman standing by the table. He knew it was Ronni, his cousin's widow, but he didn't remember her looking anywhere near this lovely. . .or fragile.

"Cole, you remember Ronni? I can't tell you how blessed I am that she agreed to move in with me after Brian passed away. This old house can get mighty lonely when you live in it by yourself."

Ronni smiled and crossed the room to hold out her hand. "Hello, Cole. Mom has been so excited about your visit."

"No more than I have about coming home. It's great to be here." He reached out and took her hand in his, noticing that her smile didn't quite reach her eyes. He couldn't really tell how she felt about him being here, but he had a feeling she wasn't quite as happy as his aunt was.

"Why don't you show Cole up to his room, Ronni, while I finish up?" His aunt turned to him. "It's your old room. It's just been updated since you last were here."

"I know right where it is, then. There's no need to bother showing me. Ronni can stay and help you. I'll be down as soon as I wash up." He took the back stairs two at a time, getting out of hearing distance just before his stomach rumbled in hunger. It'd been a long time since he'd had a home-cooked meal, and his stomach knew it.

❧

Ronni was relieved she didn't have to show Cole to his room. Somehow, she hadn't remembered him being quite so tall. . .or broad shouldered, or handsome, and she couldn't explain why her heart was pounding so fast.

"It is going to be so good to have a man around to cook for," Claudia said as she began making cream gravy to go with the chicken.

Ronni didn't quite agree with the older woman. After life with Brian, she didn't exactly miss having a man around anywhere. Intellectually, she knew that all men weren't like her late husband, but emotionally, she didn't think she'd ever trust another man with her heart. Then she wondered what that had to do with Cole.

He was here to visit with Claudia; she didn't have to worry about losing her heart to him. All she had to do was be nice to him for her mother-in-law's sake.

"This is almost ready. Would you mind putting the other dishes on the table, dear?"

"I'll be glad to." Ronni pulled the chicken from the warmer and took it to the table, and then she dished up the green beans. She eased the tray of biscuits out of the oven and placed them in a cloth-lined basket while Claudia poured the gravy into a gravy boat that'd been in her family for years.

Cole came back downstairs just as the last dish was placed on the table.

"Come on, dear," Claudia said to him. "Everything is ready."

"Oh, this smells wonderful, Aunt Claudia! I don't think I've had home-fried chicken since the last time you made it for me." He waited until she and Ronni sat down before taking his own seat.

"Will you say the blessing for us?" Claudia asked.

"I'd be glad to." He bowed his head. "Dear Lord, we thank You for this day and for the many blessings You give us. I thank You for safe travel and for this wonderful meal Aunt Claudia has prepared. Please bless her and Ronni. In Jesus' name, amen."

His prayer sounded very sincere, but Ronni wondered if Cole truly loved the Lord or if his faith was only for show as Brian's had been.

As they each helped themselves to the food, Ronni was pleased to see that Cole was definitely going to do Claudia's meal justice.

"This is wonderful, Aunt Claudia. I feel like a kid again, sitting at your kitchen table."

"I'm so glad you came for a visit."

"So am I." Cole helped himself to another piece of chicken. He grinned over at his aunt. "But not simply for the cooking. It's wonderful just to see you again and to be home. The Mississippi Coast sure has changed since I was a kid."

"Yes, it has. And those changes have hurt Magnolia Bay. But we're determined to fight back and revive this town. We can't let the casinos do any more damage to this area than they already have."

Cole wasn't sure that was possible, but he wasn't about to

voice that thought to his aunt. He could see the fire in her eyes and knew that she partially blamed the influence of the casinos for Brian's death. "I can see you've made some inroads. I noticed several new businesses in town."

"We're trying. We have to do more, though."

"If it doesn't happen, it certainly won't be from lack of trying." Ronni got up to refill their glasses with tea.

While Ronni was taking part in the conversation, Cole noted her comments seemed to be directed only to his aunt. In fact, she hadn't addressed him at all since they sat down at the table, and Cole had a feeling she wasn't too happy about his visit.

"What other avenues are you exploring?" he asked.

"Well," Aunt Claudia replied, "we want to hire a city manager, and we're thinking of ways to get the word out that we are a relaxing change from all the casino action. We just haven't quite figured out the right way to go about it yet."

"But you will," Ronnie interjected. "You have a wonderful committee that cares as much as you do about Magnolia Bay's future."

Cole liked the way Ronni tried to assure his aunt. "I'm sure you'll come up with something, Aunt Claudia. These things just take time."

"Yes, well. . ." His aunt paused and then changed the subject. "Did you see anyone you knew coming through town?"

"No. I was mostly just checking out familiar landmarks. I see my favorite ice cream parlor is now a coffee shop."

"I know. It's sad to see some of the changes. But then, there are others that are all right. It's a nice coffee shop."

Claudia smiled at him and added, "And they do have ice cream."

"I'll get out and explore a little closer tomorrow. Maybe I'll check it out."

Ronni began to clear the table. "Mom made apple pies last night. Did you save room?"

Cole leaned back in his chair and grinned. "Probably not, but that never stopped me from enjoying Aunt Claudia's apple pie in the past."

For just a minute, he thought she was going to smile at him, and he held his breath waiting to see the corners of her mouth turn up. But she turned away, and Cole was surprised at the disappointment he felt.

"Would you like coffee, too?" she asked from across the room.

"Yes, please. I take it black," he added.

"I'll help," Claudia said.

"I can get it, Mom," Ronni insisted. "You stay put. Do you want coffee with yours?"

"No, dear. It will just keep me up half the night. I'll just finish my tea with it, thank you."

Cole liked the way Ronni waited on Aunt Claudia first and then brought him a large slice of pie and a cup of coffee.

"You are having some, aren't you?" he asked Ronni.

"Oh, yes." This time she smiled at him. "*I* saved room."

He laughed and was pleased to hear her chuckle. So she wasn't super serious all the time. And she had a sense of humor.

Cole waited until she brought her own dessert to the table before forking a large bite of pie into his mouth.

Closing his eyes, he chewed and swallowed. "Mmm, this was worth the wait, Aunt Claudia."

"Thank you, dear."

The conversation turned to visits of the past as his aunt seemed to want to reminisce. Ronni got up to clear the table.

"Thank you," Cole said as she gathered up his plate and fork. "I'll help with the cleanup."

"No, I will," Claudia said.

"There's no need for either of you to help. I'll clean up," Ronni insisted. "You two need a chance to catch up. Why don't you take Cole to your study and relax, Mom?"

"I'd like to help," Cole said. He hated to leave her with all the work.

Ronni shook her head but then conceded. "You can help another time."

"You promise?" Cole was surprised to see the color rise on her cheeks, and she inclined her head. . .just slightly. He hoped he hadn't made her mad.

"All right, then. Let's go, Aunt Claudia."

His aunt took her tea glass to the sink and gave Ronni a hug. "Thank you."

"You're welcome. Enjoy your visit," Ronni said.

His aunt crossed the room and motioned to him to follow. Now was the time to find out what it was that had Aunt Claudia so worried. It certainly seemed that Ronni was unaware of the problems, but Cole wondered if she might somehow be part of them.

❧

Ronni breathed a sigh of relief as they left the room. Was it possible the man was as nice as he seemed? Cole was very considerate of Claudia, and he had wonderful manners. She shook her head as she went about cleaning up the kitchen. Maybe he was just on his best behavior around Claudia. In any case, she hoped he wouldn't be staying too long. . . . She felt entirely too unsettled with him here.

She wiped down the counters and the table and then started the dishwasher. After putting the coffee on for the next morning, she left a light on over the stove and went upstairs. It had been a long day, and she was tired.

A long soak helped relax her, and by the time she read her Bible, she was feeling better about Cole's visit. After all, he was here to see Claudia, and his visit seemed to be just what she needed. Ronni told herself she should be grateful that he'd come.

She turned out the bedside lamp and said her prayers. "Dear Lord, thank You for all my many blessings. Thank You for Mom. . .and for Cole's visit giving her a lift. Please help me to make him feel comfortable here for her sake. And please help me not to show them both that what I'd really like is for him to go back to Texas. And forgive me for feeling that way. Your will be done, Lord. I thank You most of all for Your precious Son and our Savior, Jesus Christ. In His name, I pray, amen."

≈

Cole took a seat in the leather club chair that sat across from the matching one his aunt was sitting in and took the papers she handed him. He looked over the final payment notices she'd received on accounts she had never opened and at her current bank statement. His aunt had been right; something was very wrong. The payment notices were from companies she'd done business with in the past, but she was certain she'd paid them off long ago and hadn't charged anything else.

The bank statements were in total disarray, and he could tell she'd unsuccessfully tried to balance them. He didn't know where the problem was, but he was going to get to the bottom of it all.

"Try not to worry, Aunt Claudia. We'll try to get it all straightened out, I promise."

His aunt sighed deeply and leaned back in her chair, closing her eyes. "Thank you, Cole. I just don't know what happened, but I do know I need your help in making things right. I've never been much of a money manager. Your uncle Drew took care of those things. But sadly, he wasn't very good at it, either. To tell the truth, the Melrose family hasn't been one of the wealthiest families in the area for a good while. I just didn't realize how bad it was while Drew was alive, and then. . .Brian offered to help with the finances."

Claudia looked at Cole with tears in her eyes. "What can I say? He was my son, and I trusted him." She sighed and shook her head. "If these debts lead back to Brian, I will have to pay them. . .some way. But please help me find a way to keep the house, Cole."

He didn't know enough about it all to know that he could do that. He made the only promise he could. "I'll do all I can, Aunt Claudia."

"I know you will. And please don't mention any of this to Ronni—at least not yet. It was bad enough that he gambled all of their savings away. It will break her heart all over again if he's left me with nothing, too."

four

Cole sat in the study for a while after his aunt went upstairs. Even he found it hard to believe that Brian had put his mother in financial jeopardy, but that seemed to be the only answer to the mess his aunt found herself in. He still wasn't completely convinced that Ronni had nothing to do with all this, but he certainly hoped not. And he now knew how she had ended up living with Claudia. It appeared Brian hadn't left her any choice. The arrangement seemed to be working out well for both women, but he couldn't help wondering why Ronni was still here. She was young and single. Brian had been gone almost a year now. The last place most women he knew would want to live would be with their late husband's mother. Aunt Claudia was a wonderful woman, but still. . .

It was obvious that they cared for each other, and he sent up a silent prayer that Ronni wasn't involved in this financial mess. He wasn't sure his aunt Claudia could handle that news.

She had aged since Brian's death, but he could see that her involvement in trying to revive Magnolia Bay was giving her a cause and goal to work toward. He prayed that the town would have good results from all the hard work she and her committee were doing.

Feeling like he needed to stretch his legs, Cole let himself out the back door. The moon was large and bright, and the February night was quite cool. He grabbed a jacket he'd left in his car and took a walk on the trail he remembered from his boyhood visits. It was a beautiful piece of property, and he hoped his aunt wasn't in danger of actually losing it. Tomorrow, he'd go over her papers again in depth and begin to check with all the creditors she'd been receiving bills from. There had to be an answer to all of this.

As he turned and started back toward the house, he could see lights upstairs. He knew where his aunt's room was. The other must be Ronni's. He'd never been married, and he could only imagine how lonely it would be when one lost the person they loved. But how horrible it must have been for Ronni to find out that Brian hadn't cared enough to make sure she was taken care of in the event of his death. Instead, he'd gambled away everything. Ronni was a lovely woman. Cole's hand clenched into a fist. It was just a good thing his cousin wasn't standing in front of him now.

&a

Ronni had set her alarm for thirty minutes earlier than normal, hoping to get dressed for work and out the door before Claudia or Cole came downstairs. She'd grab something to eat at the coffee shop downtown.

But as she went downstairs, the smell of bacon frying told her she wasn't going to be so lucky. She entered the kitchen and saw Cole sitting at the table with a cup of coffee, while Claudia stood at the stove.

Cole looked up just as she stepped into the room. "Good morning." He smiled.

"Good morning." Ronni wasn't sure what to say next.

"Would you like an omelet, Ronni?" Claudia asked,

looking fresh and rested. . .better than she had in months, actually. "I'm making one for Cole."

Ronni loved Claudia's omelets. They were always light and fluffy, filled with cheese and onions. Much as she would like to have one, what she really wanted was to escape Cole's close scrutiny. She was pretty sure he was watching her from the way the back of her neck prickled, and she was glad she had a good excuse to get to work early. "No, thank you. Much as I'd like to have one, I'll just take a bacon sandwich and some coffee with me. We received a lot of stock yesterday, and I want to help get it out on the floor before opening."

She popped a piece of bread in the toaster and poured coffee in a travel cup. Once the toast was ready, she plucked a couple pieces of bacon, laid them on the golden brown bread, and folded it over.

"I understand, but that's not much of a breakfast," Claudia said.

"It's enough. But thank you, Mom," she added, giving the older woman a kiss on the cheek. "You know I love your omelets."

"I do."

Ronni glanced over at Cole on her way out the door, only to find that he was leaning back in his chair, watching her as she suspected. He smiled again, and her heart did a funny little jump in her chest. She sloshed her coffee a bit and was glad it had a lid to catch the warm liquid. She felt she had to say something before walking out the door. "You two have a good day."

"You, too," Cole said as he got up and opened the door for her.

She did have her hands full with the sandwich that was getting cold, the coffee cup, and her purse, and she appreciated his help. "Thank you."

He looked into her eyes and inclined his head. "You are welcome."

The breath caught in Ronni's throat, and it wasn't until the door shut behind her that she could let it out. He was one nice-looking man. His hair was light brown, and his eyes were the color of cinnamon. She was spending *way* too much time thinking about Cole Bannister, she told herself as she got in the car and started it up. Hadn't she decided never to let herself become interested in anyone again? And wasn't she determined that she'd not let her happiness or her livelihood depend on another man. . .ever again?

"Yes!" Ronni answered her thoughts out loud.

Besides, his visit had nothing to do with her and everything to do with Claudia, she told herself. She really knew nothing about him, but his consideration of Claudia and the obvious love they felt for one another had gone a long way in convincing Ronni that his visit would be good for her mother-in-law. . .if uncomfortable for her. She'd just try to avoid being around him as much as she could while he was here.

She was at the shop a full hour before Meagan arrived. The newlywed rarely came in early anymore, wanting to see her husband off to work and his younger sister, who they were helping to raise, off to school.

Meagan breezed in and saw that Ronni had been hard at work for a while. "What? Did you get up at sunrise to get here?"

Ronni chuckled and shook her head. "No. But I wanted to get out of the house this morning, and I figured I could put the extra time to good use."

"What's wrong at home?" Meagan asked, leaning against the counter.

"Nothing." Ronni wished she hadn't said anything about not wanting to be at home. "I just kind of feel out of place around Claudia's nephew."

"Cole? Cole Bannister is here? Oh, Ronni, Cole is such a nice person. There's no need to feel uncomfortable around him."

Ronni shrugged. It was fine for Meagan to say. Her pulse didn't take off in a gallop when the man smiled at her. "Well, he and Claudia haven't seen each other in a while. I thought they might need some time without me there."

"Well, maybe. But don't you think for a moment that Cole is someone to avoid. We've been friends a long time," Meagan said before she disappeared down the hall and into the small kitchen where they kept a coffeepot.

"Really?" Ronni followed her into the room. "How did you two meet?"

Meagan poured them both a cup of the coffee Ronni had put on earlier. She took a seat at the small table. Ronni sat down across from her and waited.

"I first met Cole when he came to spend the summers with Claudia after his mom passed away. You know, Claudia and my gram were friends. Anyway, we ran into each other a lot when he was here. But it was later, after we were grown, that I really got to know him."

"Oh?" Ronni couldn't help but be curious.

Meagan nodded and took a sip of coffee before explaining. "He lived in Dallas, and we attended the same church. It was wonderful to have that connection to home. Just you wait until you get to know him better. He's really a great guy!"

Ronni didn't comment.

"I got to know him much better in Dallas than on his visits here. From what I do remember, though, he always seemed a little lonely here. I don't think he and Brian were all that close."

Somehow that didn't surprise Ronni.

"Oh! Mom and Dad are coming down for the weekend. I need to go check out the apartment and make sure it's ready for them," Meagan said, draining her coffee cup and putting it in the small sink.

"Do you need any help?"

"No. I'm sure it's all okay. I just want to air it out a little. I am so glad that they have started using it for visits. It's not but about an hour up to their place, but with Nick's work and Tori's school and all, it just makes it easier on us to see them more often."

Meagan had lived in the apartment over the shop when she first came back to Magnolia Bay, and after she and Nick got married, they had offered the apartment to Ronni. But she hadn't wanted to leave Claudia all alone.

"Try to get to know Cole, Ronni. You'll see I'm right about him," Meagan said before hurrying up the staircase to check on the apartment.

Ronni looked at her watch. It was time. She went to turn the sign in the window to OPEN. Maybe she should take Meagan's advice about Cole. At the very least, maybe she should wait a while before forming any opinions about him.

❧

Cole took the last bite of omelet and leaned back in his chair. "Aunt Claudia, I'm going to gain a ton if you keep feeding me like this."

She chuckled and shook her head. "I don't think so. But there's always the walking trail out back if you think you must work it off. You could do a little jogging. I intend to feed you as many of your favorites as I can while you are here."

"Well, I'll just make use of that track then, 'cause I sure don't want to miss out on your home cooking."

"Ronni is a very good cook, too," his aunt said.

Cole had been trying to put his cousin's widow out of his mind ever since she had walked out the door, but mention of her name showed him that he hadn't been very successful. He'd been surprised at how immediately attracted to her he was. She was very pretty with her auburn hair and hazel eyes, but it was more than her looks. There was something about her that had kept her in his thoughts since last night. . .and he'd been thinking about the way soft color had crept up her cheeks as she walked past him on her way out this morning. He just hoped it wasn't from anger. He had the distinct feeling she didn't want him here. . .or something. She seemed wary of him, and he couldn't figure out why.

"Aunt Claudia, I guess she's living with you because of the debt Brian left her in?"

The pained expression in his aunt's eyes told him before she uttered a word. "Yes. She tried not to let me know, but when the bank foreclosed on their condo, it became pretty obvious."

"I'm sure she was grateful for your invitation to come live here."

Claudia shook her head. "It took awhile to convince her. I thought she was going to move into the apartment above Meagan's Color Cottage at first. But finally, I was able to convince her of how lonely it was living here all alone, and she agreed to move in."

"Aunt Claudia, do you think she might have something to do with—"

"No! Ronni would never do something like that."

"I hope not." Cole just couldn't figure out how Brian could have caused all of this mess his aunt was in. But he prayed that Aunt Claudia was right and that Ronni didn't have anything to do with it.

"Cole, Ronni became a Christian after she married Brian. He didn't go to church like he should have, but she went with me even when he didn't. And she's been a source of strength to me in the last year."

He could hear the tears in his aunt's voice. "I'm sorry, Aunt Claudia. I didn't mean to upset you."

"I know you didn't, dear." She dabbed at her eyes with her napkin. "Just wait until you get to know her better. You'll discover that she's a wonderful woman. I don't know what I would have done without her since Brian died. I really don't."

"But you haven't told her that you are in financial trouble." He took a sip of coffee and waited for his aunt's answer.

"No." Aunt Claudia shook her head. "I don't want to worry her. . .and I don't want to bring her more heartache."

"But that's almost inevitable, isn't it?"

His aunt rubbed a hand over her brow and sighed, deeply. "I suppose. I just hate to—"

"Aunt Claudia, wouldn't she be more upset thinking you kept it from her?"

"I hadn't thought of it that way."

"I have a feeling she would want to know."

Claudia got up to clear the table. "All right. I'll tell her tonight."

"Good. I think you'll feel better after you do."

"You are probably right."

Cole stood up and took the dishes from her. "I'll help. And, Aunt Claudia, you know I don't want either you or Ronni to suffer any more heartache than you already have endured, don't you?"

"Of course I do. I'm just afraid more is coming our way, and there's nothing any of us can do about it."

five

Cole spent the better part of the afternoon and into early evening going over his aunt's papers more closely than he'd been able to the night before. He was puzzled by some of the charges that had been made to her and began to make a list of questions to ask her about. It appeared some furniture had been purchased a couple of months before Brian died—evidently on a deferred-payment schedule of some kind—but now it was due, and so was the interest, as no payments had been made.

Jewelry had been charged at a well-known jewelry store in Mobile, Alabama, in a similar fashion. And many pieces of expensive ladies' apparel had been charged to his aunt's accounts at various stores. He wanted to make certain that she hadn't just forgotten about some of these purchases.

It appeared that a lot of money had been taken out of her savings account, but what had him really uneasy was that it seemed a large loan had been taken out with one of those national lending companies that advertised on television all the time and that the house had been put up as collateral. That could present a serious problem for his aunt.

He made a list of who he needed to make appointments with and those businesses that he wanted to try to get detailed copies of the receipts from. Hopefully, he'd have a better understanding of the extent of the problem in a few days. But it didn't look good at all.

Cole sighed and stood up to stretch. If his aunt wasn't responsible, it could only boil down to Brian. . .or possibly Ronni. But he found himself hoping and praying that it wasn't her. When he came out of the study, he found his aunt in the kitchen stirring up some wonderful aromas. If his nose wasn't deceiving him, they were having pot roast for supper.

She handed him a cup of coffee. "You've been going over those papers for a long time, and I know how frustrating that is."

"Now I know why you sounded so confused on the phone the other day." He rubbed the back of his neck, twisting and turning it, trying to get the kinks out.

"Have you come to any conclusions?"

"No," Cole shook his head and took a drink of the fragrant liquid. "I hope to have a better grip on it all in a few days."

"I just can't thank you enough for coming to help me out, Cole. I didn't know where to begin."

"Well, I'm determined to get to the bottom of it all, Aunt Claudia. It may take a little longer than we'd like, but we'll figure it all out. Try not to worry." He sniffed and changed the subject. "It smells wonderful in here. I didn't realize I was hungry until I came into this room."

"Well, why don't you take that cup of coffee outside and get some fresh air? Ronni had a few errands to run after work; but she'll be showing up any minute now, and we'll eat shortly."

"Can I help do anything?" Cole asked, although it looked like his aunt had everything under control. Even the table was set.

"No, dear. Thank you. You go on out and wait for Ronni while I finish up."

"Yes, ma'am." Cole headed out the back door as ordered. He took a seat in one of the chaise lounges and cupped his mug with both hands. The sun had set, and it was cool out. But the coffee warmed him, and he let himself relax as best he could.

He couldn't pretend that he wasn't a little apprehensive about what Ronni's reaction would be when Claudia told her about the financial mess she was in. He truly hated for either of them to go through any more anguish than they already had, but like his aunt, he had a feeling there was more to come. When car lights alerted him to Ronni's arrival, he got to his feet and went to meet her.

"Good evening, Ronni," he said, opening the car door for her. "Aunt Claudia banished me from the kitchen, but I think I can safely reenter if I'm with you."

He was rewarded with a soft chuckle as she got out of the car. "I think you'll have to come up with something better than that. Mom never runs people out of her kitchen."

"Well. . .maybe banished was too strong a word. She suggested I have my coffee outside." He waved his cup in the air to back up his words.

"Hmm. Did you make her angry?" They started walking toward the house.

"I don't think so. I think she thought I was going to ask for a sampling of that pot roast and ruin my appetite for the rest of the meal. She used to admonish Brian and me not to spoil our appetites right before supper."

Cole could have bit his tongue. At the mention of Brian's

name, Ronni's light mood seemed to change.

"That sounds like Mom" was all she said as they entered the kitchen.

"What sounds like me?" Claudia turned from taking fluffy homemade rolls from the oven.

"Making sure no one loses their appetite before a meal."

Claudia laughed. "That's right. I figure my cooking tastes even better when one is starving."

Ronni laid her purse on the counter and washed her hands at the sink. "Let me help you get things on the table."

"I can help, too," Cole offered, taking the large bowl of mashed potatoes in hand. "The quicker we get it to the table, the better."

"I don't think I have to worry about Cole liking this meal," Claudia said in a whisper loud enough for him to hear.

"No." He grinned at her. "That's something you definitely don't have to worry about." He took the carrots to the table while Ronni and his aunt brought the roast, gravy, and bread. When the women were seated, he took his own chair.

He said the blessing and sent up a silent addition to it that Claudia would be able to tell Ronni why he was here and about the financial trouble she found herself in, and that Ronni. . .he truly didn't know what to ask for Ronni. That she wouldn't be too upset. That she would be supportive of Aunt Claudia, and—especially—that she had nothing to do with the problem.

Ronni was quiet at first, listening to his and Claudia's conversation, but near the end of the meal, his aunt drew her into the conversation by asking about her day and how

Meagan liked being a newlywed.

"She loves it. And I've never seen her look better. I'm so glad she opened a shop here and that she and Nick could get back together."

"Well, Dallas sure misses her," Cole said. "I'm glad she's happy, though. You know she was almost engaged to a friend of mine from church there. . .Thad Cameron."

"That's right. I didn't realize you knew him," Ronni answered. "He seemed like a really nice man."

"He is. One of the best."

"How's he doing?" Claudia asked.

Cole shrugged. "He's okay. I guess it wasn't easy for him to realize Meagan was in love with someone else, but he said he wished her well."

"It's sad someone had to get hurt. Hopefully, he'll find someone just right for him one of these days." Claudia dabbed the corner of her mouth with a napkin. "Are you two ready for dessert?"

"Oh. . .I ate so much; I think I'll wait until later, if that's okay, Aunt Claudia."

"Me, too, Mom."

Claudia nodded. "We can have it later then. Ronni, would you join Cole and me in the study after we clean up? I need to discuss something with you."

Ronni looked a little puzzled to Cole, but she agreed quickly enough. "Of course."

Tonight, no one told him he couldn't help, and they all made quick work of cleaning up the kitchen.

"I'll put on a fresh pot of coffee, and we can have it with the pie later," Claudia said as Ronni wiped down the counters.

"I'll go get a few papers together, Aunt Claudia," Cole said.

"We'll be right there, dear."

He didn't wait to hear Ronni's response. He just headed for the study and straightened up some of the paperwork he had lying on the desk, before picking up a few sheets he'd made notes on and taking a seat in the same chair he'd occupied the night before. He really was dreading this next hour or so for his aunt and wanted to make it as easy on her as he could.

When Ronni and his aunt came in a few minutes later, he could tell Ronni was uneasy. But Aunt Claudia seemed determined as she asked Ronni to sit beside her on the leather couch facing the fireplace.

"Ronni, dear, there's something I need to tell you." Claudia paused and took a deep breath. "Cole told me you need to know, and he's right. I just haven't wanted to upset you—"

"What is it, Mom? Have I done something to trouble you?"

"Oh no, Ronni! You've done nothing. But we have a problem, and I asked Cole to come see if he could help figure it out."

Ronni's glance strayed to Cole as she asked, "What is it? What's wrong?"

"I am in deep trouble financially. I'm not sure how bad it is just yet, but it is serious."

"Oh, Mom. I'm sorry. I—"

Cole could see that she was both sincere in her compassion and surprised by Claudia's admission.

"It's not your fault, dear. But I suspect Brian might have

had something to do with it."

"Brian? How could he. . .I mean, he's been gone—"

"Some of the things that were charged to my name were done on one of those deferred-payment plans. You know, no interest, no payments for a year or two?"

"Oh."

"Well, it appears that they are due now. And a substantial amount of money has been taken out of my savings account. It was done before Brian passed away, but I didn't discover it until a few months ago. I usually throw my statements in the desk when I get them and look them over when I get to it. With Brian's death and all, well, I fell really far behind. But I wasn't concerned about it. It wasn't as if I was using any of the money.

"But how?"

"I don't know. And maybe Brian didn't have anything to do it. It could be a case of having my identity stolen, I suppose. But I. . ." Claudia shook her head. "There's more."

"More?" Ronni asked incredulously.

Observing Ronni's reactions, Cole felt some of the tension in his neck ease, sensing more and more that Ronni didn't have anything to do with it all.

"Cole, you tell her, please."

He nodded and turned to Ronni. "It also appears that a huge loan was taken out in Aunt Claudia's name with the house put up as collateral."

"No! How could that happen?" Ronni jumped to her feet and began to pace the floor in front of the fireplace. "Surely Brian wouldn't have done that to you, Mom! Not to you!"

"Oh, Ronni. I am so sorry, dear." Claudia jumped up

and pulled the younger woman into a hug. "I didn't want to upset you about all this. That's why I haven't told you before now."

"I thought she should tell you, Ronni. It's my fault—"

She shook her head as she hugged Aunt Claudia back. "Don't apologize, please. I'm just upset on your account. And Cole was right. I wish you'd told me before now so I could have tried to help. . .or at least shared the burden with you."

Claudia wiped at the tears in her eyes. "I never doubted that you would be there for me, Ronni. I. . .if Brian had anything to do with this. . .I just didn't want to bring you more pain."

"But what about you, Mom? I think you've suffered enough, too."

Claudia sighed. "Well, Cole has come to help us figure out what is going on. It looks like I could lose the family home, Ronni. He's going to see if he can help us keep it, aren't you, dear?"

"I'm going to do all I can." He wished he could take the stricken look off Ronni's face. He was quite sure that she knew nothing of Claudia's troubles and was more relieved than he cared to reflect about at the moment. "Let's go get that coffee, okay? I have a few things I want to run by you both."

"Yes, yes," Claudia agreed. "Let's do that."

After fixing their coffees, they gathered around the kitchen table; he spread out the papers he'd brought with him. "I'm a bit puzzled by several things—the first being a series of charges at these stores for quite a few outfits. Are you sure you just didn't forget buying these things, Aunt Claudia?"

She took the statements he handed her and studied them. "I'm sure. I haven't shopped at these stores in a long time." She shook her head as she looked closer at one of the statements and then back at Cole. "I'm certain. This store does a detailed accounting, and none of these things are my size, Cole."

Ronni reached out and took the statement from her. After studying it for a few minutes, she nodded. "Mom is right. And just in case you were wondering if she bought these things for me, they aren't my size, either."

Cole certainly wasn't going to mention that the question had entered his mind. "That's what I needed to know. It appears there's been a mistake on the part of the clothing store. I'll check with them tomorrow. And I'll call the company that issued the loan, Aunt Claudia. We will get to the bottom of this. I promise."

"Thank you. And thank you for insisting I tell Ronni." She reached over and patted her daughter-in-law's hand. "I feel so much better now that you know."

"I'm glad. I. . ." Ronni seemed to think better of what she'd been about to say and changed the subject completely. "How about that pie now? Anyone got room?"

"I certainly do," Cole said, feeling like there was hope that he might find out things weren't quite as bad as he and his aunt had first thought. Obviously there was some mistake with the clothing charges. For tonight, he'd let his aunt and Ronni hope that the rest of this mess would be due to one huge mistake, too. At least for tonight.

❧

Ronni was thankful when she could finally excuse herself and go up to her room. Even after going over the conversation while she showered and got ready for bed, she still couldn't grasp all that Claudia had told her. How could her finances possibly be in such trouble, and how could Brian have had anything to do with it? The thought that he might have gave birth to a white-hot anger all over again. It was bad enough that he'd left her penniless; surely he wouldn't have done the same thing to his mother.

And Ronni was angry with herself for not realizing sooner that Claudia was having problems. She should have put two and two together when Claudia finally agreed to let her regular housekeeper come in only once a month. If she'd known earlier, maybe she could have done something. But what? Much as she wished Claudia hadn't had to turn to Cole for help—she had a feeling he didn't trust her any more than she trusted him—she was glad he was here. She didn't have any idea how to handle this kind of problem, and if Cole could help Claudia keep her family home, Ronni would do all she could to help. And be thankful that he came. She'd try.

She read her Bible and tried to put all the thoughts of Brian and the hurt he'd caused her out of her mind. She was getting over it all; she really was. This just brought it all back to mind. But with the Lord's help, she and Claudia would get through all of this, too.

"Dear Lord, please be with Mom tonight and comfort her. I pray she feels better now that she has told me about her troubles and has Cole here to help. And I pray that You will show him just what to do to help her. Please take this anger I feel for Brian away from me again. He may not have anything to do with all of this. I hope not, more for Mom's sake than mine. And please, dear Lord, help me to deal with whatever comes. In Jesus' name, I pray, amen."

&

Cole was making good use of the walking trail once more. But exercising wasn't why he was outside tonight. He was trying to convince himself that he'd been right in persuading his aunt to tell Ronni about her financial troubles, but as he recalled the look on Ronni's face when Aunt Claudia had told her, he had his doubts.

Ronni had looked truly devastated by the news that Brian might be responsible for the debt Aunt Claudia found herself in. But Ronni's hurt seemed more for Claudia than for herself, and Cole was truly touched that Ronni cared so much for his aunt.

He still couldn't figure out how Brian could have managed to do so much damage to his mother's finances without her knowledge, but he was going to find out. If he had to hire an attorney, a private investigator—whatever it took—he'd do it. He made the turn and headed back toward the house. Both upstairs lights had gone off. He hoped his aunt was able to sleep better after talking to Ronni. And he hoped Ronni didn't toss and turn all night from learning about the problem.

He sent up a silent prayer that the Lord would help them to sleep and help him to find out just how bad things were—and help Aunt Claudia keep her home.

six

The next few days were busy ones for Cole. Hard as he tried, he had little success in contacting the people he needed to talk to. He was able to get the national lending company to fax him copies of the loan that had been taken out on the house in his aunt's name, but at the end of the day, he had no more answers than when he'd started. Although she'd never done business with them before, the papers looked legitimate. And his aunt's signature was on them, with the family home put up as collateral. He did manage to buy Claudia a little more time—once he mentioned the word *fraud* and that he was going to hire an attorney—but that was about it.

Meeting his aunt for lunch at the coffee shop, he discussed what he felt their next action should be. "I don't think I'm going to be able to get the answers we need, Aunt Claudia. I'm not your legal representative, and most of the companies I've talked to aren't inclined to give me any more information than we already have."

"What do you suggest we do?"

"I think it's time we hire an attorney or investigator to get us more information. What lawyer would you recommend? Do you have one that you use?"

"Oh, Cole. I haven't needed any legal work done in a long time. The lawyer your uncle and I used passed away a year or two back." She sighed. "Maybe we could ask Nick

Chambers if he would help."

"Meagan's husband." Cole nodded. "Yes, that sounds good. I'll see if I can make us an appointment to see him as soon as possible, all right?"

"Yes. The sooner we can get this settled, the better I'll feel."

So will I. It was hard to stay upbeat about everything when he didn't seem to be getting anywhere and when he knew his aunt was expecting him to come up with some answers. Cole tried to reassure her now. "It will all work out, Aunt Claudia."

He prayed he was right as he and his aunt parted company.

❧

Ronni spent an almost-sleepless night wondering if Brian had put his mother in such a perilous situation, or if not, who else could—or even would—have. Each time she woke up, she prayed that the Lord would help them through whatever Cole found out.

When she went in to work and headed straight for the kitchen to get some aspirin, Meagan followed and looked at her closely before commenting, "You look really tired, Ronni. Are you coming down with something?"

Ronni shook her head as she swallowed the pills. "No. I don't think so. I just didn't sleep very well last night. It seems that Cole is here to help Claudia out of a financial bind that Brian might have put her in before he died. I just kept thinking about it, trying to come up with some answers each time I woke up."

"Brian? But how?" Meagan asked.

"We don't know. It appears he borrowed money in her

name and charged all kinds of things to her accounts." Ronni poured herself a cup of coffee. "Hopefully, Cole will be able to get to the bottom of it all, and it won't be as bad as we think it might be."

"Did Claudia just find out about this?" Meagan poured herself a cup of coffee and leaned against the counter.

"I think she's known for a while. . .but she didn't want to tell me unless she had to. Cole convinced her that I should know."

"You know, I seem to remember that Cole used to always be cleaning up after Brian when he came here for the summer. It appears he's having to do it again." She slapped a hand over her mouth as soon as the words were out. "I'm so sorry, Ronni. I was thinking out loud. I shouldn't have said anything—"

"Don't worry about it, Meagan. It's okay."

"But he was your husband, and I'm sure thinking he might have hurt Claudia like that is very hard on you."

"It is. And it brings up a lot of bad memories." Ronni sighed and rubbed her temple. She didn't want to think of any of it now—not of how he'd changed the day she'd been baptized or the way he'd stayed out late drinking and gambling all of their money away until the night of the accident that took his life. "It was bad enough that he left me with nothing. To think that he might have put Mom in a similar position breaks my heart."

"Well, maybe he didn't have anything to do with it. . . and Cole will find out that it's all just a huge mistake."

"We can hope, I guess," Ronni said, even though she had a feeling that Meagan didn't think that was going to be the case anymore than she did.

"I'll be praying."

Ronni smiled. "So will I. And I know He'll help us through. I just—"

"I know," Meagan interrupted. "You were just beginning to think the pain was behind you."

Ronni nodded. What could she say? Today certainly wasn't a "feels like spring" day.

❧

By that evening, Cole was feeling better about things. He'd been able to see Nick Chambers that afternoon and had retained him on behalf of his aunt. Nick had assured him that they would get copies of all the paperwork pertaining to the loan and he'd get copies of as many of the original receipts for everything as he could. They had to find out whose signature was on those charges. Cole had also given Nick the go-ahead to hire an investigator if needed, saying he would pay for all of it out of his own pocket.

He finally convinced his aunt and Ronni that it was his turn to treat for a meal, and they enjoyed a wonderful dinner at the Seaside Surf and Turf, one of the new businesses in town. Enjoying a second cup of coffee, Cole looked around at the restaurant's decor. "This is nice. I have been very impressed by the locals' determination and efforts to try to revive Magnolia Bay and not give in to the big casinos."

"It's wonderful to see new shops and businesses such as this open up," Claudia said. "We have a long way to go, but if we keep at it, we'll be a growing, thriving town once more."

Cole hoped so. He'd like to see it more the way it was when he was growing up. He took a sip of his coffee and leaned back in his chair. "Nick Chambers has agreed to help us out, Aunt Claudia. As your legal representative, he can talk to the people who are giving me the runaround. I've told him to hire an investigator if he needs to."

"Thank you, dear. Nick is a good man. I'm sure he'll do all he can for us."

Ronni said nothing, but she reached out and patted Claudia's hand. He was glad his aunt had her for support—especially since he would have to be going back and forth to Dallas.

"I know waiting won't be easy. Hopefully, we'll have more answers soon. But I have to go back to Dallas and tie up a few things. I'll be leaving tomorrow after church, but I'll be back in a few days."

"I'm sorry, Cole. I didn't mean for this to be some long-term thing you had to deal with. I know you have a business to run."

"Don't worry about it, Aunt Claudia. I wouldn't be going back to Texas now if I didn't have to. I want to get to the bottom of all of this almost as bad as you do. As soon as I take care of a few things, I'll be back. Nick has promised to let us know as soon as he has any news that can shed light on all of this. And if you need anything, I'll be just a phone call away."

"I'll make sure she's all right," Ronni said. "We've been taking care of each other for a while now."

"Yes, we have," Claudia agreed. "I don't think Cole meant—"

"I meant that if either of you find out anything you think I should know, please just give me a call. I'm very thankful you have each other." Cole tried to assure Ronni, thinking he'd put his foot in his mouth one more time. He seemed to be making a habit of that around her.

❧

Cole left for Dallas the next day. He'd accompanied them to church and stayed for the Sunday dinner Claudia had put on that morning, but he had to leave right afterward so that he could make his flight back to Texas.

Ronni and Claudia walked out to the car with him to tell him good-bye.

"I'll be back on Friday evening. If Nick gets any new information for us, he said he'd let me know immediately. In the meantime, try not to worry, okay?" He hugged his aunt.

Claudia stood on tiptoe to kiss his cheek. "I'll try. I feel so much better, knowing that you and Ronni both know about all of this. And I'm sure Nick will help all he can, too. I just want to keep the house if there is some way to do so."

"Aunt Claudia, it may not be as bad as you think. Let's wait and see what Nick can find out for us. We'll take it from there."

He got into his rental car, rolled down the window, and looked into Ronni's eyes. "I know Ronni will take good care of you." He handed her a slip of paper. "These are the numbers I can be reached at—home, work, or my cell. Call if you need me for anything, all right?"

Ronni's heart lurched as she met his gaze, and all she could do was nod.

"See you Friday," he said before turning the ignition. He gave a wave as he put the car in gear and started down the drive.

Ronni was surprised at the sense of loss she felt as Cole drove away. In only a few days, he'd managed to lift Claudia's mood. And much as she hated to admit it, he seemed to fill the house with his presence. He was considerate and caring toward Claudia. . .and toward her, too, Ronni conceded. But she still wasn't happy that they had to turn to a man for help right now. Maybe she could relax now that he was gone, and things would get back to normal.

"I'm already missing him," Claudia said as they turned to go back inside. "I'm just so glad he's helping me with this, Ronni. I really didn't know what to do."

"I know." Ronni put an arm around her shoulders. "I just wish you'd told me about it all; I could have shared the worry with you."

Claudia shook her head. "You've had more than your share of worry and pain, dear. But I am glad you know. I just hope that we have a place to live once this is over."

"I'm sure we will, Mom. Please try not to worry. At least not until we know more."

"I'll try."

As they worked together to clean up the kitchen, Ronni sent up a silent prayer that the Lord would ease Claudia's worries. . .and her own. Not so much for herself. Or even that they would have a place to live. She was sure she could rent the apartment above Meagan's Color Cottage for them, if need be. No, her concern was over how Claudia would fare having to give up her family home and having the whole town know what Brian had done.

❧

It was a long week for Cole. He wanted to go back to Magnolia Bay, but he had several appointments he was committed to keeping; and he needed to talk to his foremen and check over the building sites that were ongoing. Once he was sure things were going as planned, he could go back and devote his attention more freely to his aunt Claudia's problems.

The first time he called to check on his aunt and see how things were going, Ronni answered the phone, and he was surprised at the jolt of pleasure he felt at the sound of her voice. From then on, each time he called, Cole hoped she would be the one to answer. But the last two times, it had been his aunt who'd picked up the receiver, and Cole didn't know how to ask to talk to Ronni when he really didn't know what he'd say to her if she came to the phone. Something about her made him want to pull her into his arms and protect her. He wanted to get her to smile, to laugh, to let go of the past and live again.

Nick called on Thursday. "I don't know how to say this, except right out, Cole. Brian was having an affair when he died, and she's the reason Aunt Claudia's finances are in such a mess."

Cole felt sick deep down in the pit of his stomach at Nick's words, and for a moment, he thought he might throw up. Fury at Brian rose swift and hard, and Cole could only wish he were there so that he could—

"I'm sorry to have to tell you how rotten Brian turned out to be, Cole," Nick continued.

"I know." Cole tried to swallow around the knot of anger in his throat. He didn't know what else to say. He couldn't quite take it all in himself. All he did know was that there was no way he was going to get that smile or laughter out of Ronni anytime soon.

"The news isn't all bad—"

"Maybe not," Cole broke in, "but it's going to break Ronni and Aunt Claudia's hearts."

"I know it is. I do think we can save the home for Claudia, but I don't know any way to shield her, or Ronni, from the betrayal they are going to feel when they find out all he did."

"Not your fault, Nick. I just appreciate that you were able to sort through it all. And relieved that you think we can get Aunt Claudia out of the financial mess. I'll be in tomorrow evening and will talk to you in the next few days."

"If you want me to explain any of this, just let me know. I'll be glad to come out to Claudia's."

"Thanks, Nick. I'll think about it and let you know."

When he got off the phone, he debated whether to call his aunt and Ronni and tell them what he'd found out that night, but they knew he was coming in the next day. . .and it wasn't news he wanted to tell them over the phone. He didn't want to tell them at all, but there was no way around it. He had to. Still, there was no sense in them tossing and turning all night. He could do enough of that for all three of them.

ža

By the time he pulled into Magnolia Bay the next afternoon, Cole was totally dreading the conversation that was coming. He'd practiced what to say over and over, and he was still no closer to knowing what words to use than he had been the night before.

When Cole's cell phone rang and he heard Nick's voice on the other end, his heart sank as he wondered if there was more bad news he was going to have to break to his aunt and Ronni.

"Cole, I've been thinking that I should be there when you talk to Claudia and Ronni. I have paperwork I need to show you all, and well, I know this isn't going to be easy for you. Since you hired me to represent Claudia, I feel like I ought to at least be there when you tell them."

Cole released a huge sigh of relief and felt he had a new best friend. "Nick, man, you don't know how happy I'll be to take you up on your offer. I've been dreading this since last night."

"I understand. I can come out there this evening, or you all can come into the office tonight or in the morning. Whatever you think will be easiest."

"Thanks, Nick. I think we need to get it over with. I already told Aunt Claudia that we'd go out to dinner. We're meeting Ronni in town. Would it be all right if we met at your office this evening about eight or eight thirty?"

"That's fine. I don't blame you for wanting to get it over with. I'll see you all then."

Cole turned into his aunt's drive and pulled up beside her car. She hurried out the kitchen door almost before he could get out of the car.

"Cole! It's so good to see you! I missed you this week."

He gave her a hug and kissed her on the cheek. "I missed you, too. What time are we meeting Ronni? Nick says he has some news for us, and I told him we would meet him in his office this evening after dinner."

"He does? Well, good, I hope. Ronni said she could meet us at the Seaside Surf and Turf at six thirty."

"Good. That will give me time to get unpacked and take

a shower." Cole was exceedingly thankful that his aunt hadn't asked if he knew what Nick had found out. And if he hurried to that shower, maybe he could avoid that eventuality. He pulled his cases out of the car and followed his aunt into the house.

seven

Ronni tried to tell herself that she was glad for Claudia's sake that Cole was back, but when she was shown to their table and Cole stood and pulled out her chair for her, her pulse told her something entirely different. It began to race the minute he smiled at her and said, "It's great to see you again, Ronni."

"I. . .thank you," she responded. She quickly picked up the menu, hoping to hide her reaction to him. She couldn't bring herself to say how wonderful it was to see him again. But it was. She'd thought about him all week and looked forward to his calls, even if all she did was say that she was doing fine, ask how he was, and call Claudia to the telephone.

After the waiter took their order, Claudia leaned across the table and said, "Nick has some news for us. We're going to meet him at his office when we leave here."

Ronni wished she'd opted for something smaller than the seafood platter she'd ordered. Suddenly her appetite seemed to be leaving. "It will be good to know something, I suppose."

Claudia nodded. "Yes, it will. Did he tell you what he'd found out, Cole?"

"He didn't go into detail, Aunt Claudia. He did say it was both good and bad news."

Ronni shrugged and said, "We'll know soon enough, I

guess." She had a feeling that Cole knew more than he was telling from the relieved expression on his face as Claudia asked no more questions.

By the time they finished their meal and drove over to Nick's office, Ronni wondered if Cole's and Claudia's stomachs were churning as much as hers was. If it turned out that Brian was responsible for his mother's troubles, she knew it wouldn't surprise her; she just worried about Claudia and the hurt she would feel.

Nick welcomed them in himself, as it was after office hours and his receptionist was gone for the day.

"Miss Claudia and Ronni, it's great to see you both." He gave them each a kiss on the cheek and shook Cole's hand. "Good to see you, too, Cole. I know you are all anxious to hear what we've found out. Come on into the conference room."

He ushered them into a room with a table large enough for them all to sit around and opened a file folder. "Miss Claudia, I do believe we'll be able to get your credit straightened out in time. That is the good news."

Ronni held her breath as she watched Claudia sit up a little straighter and lift her chin.

"And the bad news?" Claudia asked.

"I am so sorry to have to tell you, but it does appear that Brian did put your home up as collateral for the large loan. . . and forged your name to the documents."

Ronni reached for one of Claudia's hands and squeezed it as Claudia nodded at the news.

"And. . ." Nick cleared his throat, and his eyes met Ronni's. "The other charges for clothing and furniture. . . we know who those were for."

"Who they were for?"

"Yes. There is no easy way to tell you two this. Brian was buying all of these things for a woman named Belinda Marsh. Have you ever heard of her?"

Ronni shook her head. She was suddenly finding it hard to breathe, much less speak.

Claudia asked the question Ronni couldn't seem to get past her lips. "Who is this woman?"

"She works at one of the casinos. She met Brian there, and they. . ." Nick cleared his throat once more. "Evidently, they had an affair. She says he wanted to marry her. I am so sorry, Ronni."

Ronni closed her eyes against the sharp stab of pain in her chest. She'd thought she would be immune to any hurt Brian could inflict on her now that he was gone. She'd been wrong.

"Are you sure about all of this, Nick?" Claudia asked, patting Ronni's hand now.

"We've talked to her. Brian took out the loan to help her buy a condo. He charged the furniture and the clothing. She says she thought it was all on his account. And some of it may have been. Ronni, we can check on the accounts you and Brian held to see—"

"No." She forced the word out. "I—I don't know." She didn't know what to say or what to do. Nothing would change things. Not only had her husband been addicted to gambling and drinking, he'd also had an affair. The thought of it made her sick.

"This is a lot for Ronni and Aunt Claudia to take in, Nick," Cole said. "Maybe we should go home tonight and come back—"

"No! We need to know it all," Ronni insisted. "You mentioned that Mom's credit might be cleared up. What can you do for her? If there is any good news about Mom keeping her home, we need to hear it now. Please."

Nick nodded. "I understand. Ms. Marsh knows she's in trouble and that I've contacted the DA about possible charges we could bring against her. But if she's willing to help us with Miss Claudia's problem—in getting the truth out that it was not Claudia who charged those things or took out the loan, but Brian instead—I'm not sure we should bring the charges against her."

"Well, someone is going to have to pay back all that money. Is she able to do that?" Claudia asked.

"She could be forced to sell the condo and pay back the loan and then make payments on the charges."

"How will she do that if she's in prison?"

"I think she'll be glad to do whatever it takes to stay out of jail."

Claudia was silent for a moment.

"Let Nick see what he can do, Aunt Claudia," Cole said. "I believe we can get you out of this mess. You certainly shouldn't have to repay the debts Brian incurred in your name."

"I don't want the family name ruined in this area, Cole. The Melroses have been respected in this community for years. I can't let that name be tarnished. And I believe in paying debts," Claudia said, standing. "If my son is responsible for it all, and it was done in my name, then I must see that it is paid back."

"I don't think it will come to that, Miss Claudia. Let me see what I can do."

"Nick is right, Aunt Claudia. Let him check into things for us, and then we can decide how to best handle it all." Cole stood behind Ronni's chair. "Are you ready, Ronni?"

"Yes." She nodded and pushed away from the table. *Oh yes*. She was ready to get out of this room.

Nick showed them out. "I am sorry about Brian's part in all of this. I know that it has to be very painful for you both. But I also know that you'll both look to the Lord to get you through, just as you always have. It's going to be all right. He'll see to it."

She and Claudia looked at each other and nodded.

"Thank you, Nick. It's good to have that reminder." Claudia smiled at him.

"We all need one from time to time," he said. "Cole, you going to be around for a while?"

"I'm planning on it. I should be here at least a week or so before I have to check on things in Texas again."

Nick nodded. "Good. I'll be in touch with you all."

Ronni couldn't think of a thing to say as they said good-bye to Nick and made their way to their cars.

"Would you like me to ride home with you, dear?" Claudia asked.

"No, I'll be fine, Mom. You go on with Cole. I'll see you there."

"If you are sure. . . ."

Ronni kissed her on the cheek. She knew the older woman was worried about her. "I'm sure."

Claudia nodded. "We'll see you at home."

Ronni was exceedingly glad she had her own car. She didn't think she could have ridden home with Cole and Claudia. She needed some time to herself even if it was only on the drive home. She'd thought all the hurt over Brian was finally gone, but no. He'd left her with one more hurdle to jump over. And it was a big one.

Dear Lord, could I have been that bad a wife that he couldn't even be faithful to me? I loved him so when we got married. And I took our vows seriously. Even more so after I became a Christian. I tried to be the best wife I could be to him, hoping that he would give up gambling and drinking. I'm sure he was disappointed that I didn't want to share that part of life with him, but I tried to share all the rest. I was there for him, I was affectionate to him, I took care of the house, of his clothes. . .of him.

She wiped at the tears that streamed down her cheeks. Evidently her love just wasn't enough for Brian. She'd failed him in some way. Maybe she just didn't know how to be a good wife. All the pain and doubts and questions she'd dealt with after Brian's death assailed her once more. She couldn't help wondering what this Belinda Marsh was like. Yet she really didn't want to think about her.

It would have helped if the drive home were longer, and she debated whether to just keep driving past the turnoff to Melrose Manor. But Claudia would worry and probably send Cole out to look for her. There was no sense giving Claudia more to stress about. She hoped that she could hide the pain she felt from the two of them. She wanted to be able to help Brian's mother.

"Please, Lord, please help me as You always have. And please help Mom right now. I'm sure her heart is breaking for me as well as for herself. Please comfort her and help us to come up with a way to settle all of this without her losing everything. And please, just let me get through the next hour or so until I can get to my room before I break down again," she whispered.

She slowed down when she turned into the drive to give Claudia and Cole time to get into the house and for her to compose herself. By the time she parked her car and started inside the house, her tears had dried, and she thought she could hold them at bay—for now.

❧

Cole and his aunt drove home in silence. He was kind of glad that Ronni had her own car. He truly didn't know what to say to her. The look on her face when Nick had told them that Brian had been having an affair was one he'd never forget. *Devastated.* There was no other word that came to mind to describe her expression.

He looked into his rearview mirror to make sure she was behind them and was greatly relieved when she turned into the long drive behind them, but he would have understood if she'd just kept driving.

"I don't understand how my son could have done the things Brian did, Cole," Claudia said.

"I know, Aunt Claudia. I don't, either." And he didn't. He particularly couldn't fathom how Brian could have been untrue to his wife. It just didn't make any sense. His aunt had looked totally distraught at the news of Brian's betrayal to herself and especially to Ronni, and Cole was certain her heart was breaking for her daughter-in-law.

"The hardest thing to accept about all of this is that he was unfaithful to Ronni." His aunt sighed deeply and shook her head. "I don't know how he could have done that to her. She was crazy about him when they got married. She was a wonderful Christian wife for him. And she's always been loving and giving and kind. . . ." Her voice trailed off.

The silence left Cole with his own thoughts. He could remember how crazy Brian and Ronni had seemed about each other at their wedding. He couldn't help but wonder what had happened. Of course he knew Brian—in some ways better than his aunt had. Brian liked to drink, and Cole knew he'd been caught up in gambling. Evidently Brian hadn't loved Ronni enough to let her love for him change him. For Brian to have treated her so shabbily was something he'd never understand.

What a wasted life his cousin had lived.

They pulled into the drive. For a minute he thought he might wait for Ronni, but then he decided to go on inside. She might need some time to herself, and he didn't want her to feel uncomfortable if she wasn't ready to talk about the situation with him around.

He followed his aunt inside but stood by the kitchen window to make sure Ronni hadn't changed her mind and gone back into town.

"She was right behind us, wasn't she?" his aunt asked as she put the teakettle on.

"Yes." He could see her headlights rounding the curved drive before he heard the car, and he was a little surprised at the relief he felt knowing she was there. "Here she is now."

Cole fought the urge to meet her outside and settled for opening the kitchen door for her instead. He could tell she'd been crying and had a feeling it wouldn't take much for her to start up again.

"Thank you," she said, quickly taking off her jacket and laying her purse down. She crossed over to Claudia, put an arm around her shoulders, and gave her a quick hug. "Oh good, Mom. I was hoping for a cup of tea to go upstairs with."

They busied themselves with tea bags and cups and saucers.

"Would you like a cup of tea, Cole?" his aunt asked.

"No, thank you. I'm fine." The kettle started to whistle, and he watched them brew the tea. He started to take a seat at the table but hesitated, unsure of whether he should stay there or slip upstairs so that the two women could have some time alone. Ronni made his mind up for him as she took her cup of tea in hand and headed toward the stairs. "I'll let you two catch up and see you tomorrow, all right?"

"See you in the morning, dear." Claudia brought her cup over and joined Cole at the table.

"See you then," Ronni said.

"Good night, Ronni," Cole said, taking a seat at the table.

"Night." For one second her gaze met his before she climbed the stairs. He could see the unshed tears just before she turned away. He wanted to say so much to her. To tell her Brian was crazy. To tell her that he wished he could ease her pain. To tell her that he was beginning to care for her. . .a lot. But now was certainly not the time.

❧

Ronni barely made it to the landing before the tears began flowing again. She didn't know who she was crying for— herself or Claudia. Were her tears for what was or for what could have been?

When she got to her room, she set down the tea and ran

to get a box of tissues. Dropping down in her easy chair, she wiped her eyes once more and blew her nose. She took a sip of tea and sniffed. Tears streamed once more. She sipped her tea and tried not to cry in it. But finally, she gave into the sobs that no longer could be suppressed.

Eventually, the shock and pain began to ease. She'd known Brian hadn't loved her the way she loved him. . . at least not at the end. If she was truthful with herself, she'd wondered from time to time if there was someone else—and then felt guilty for not trusting him. Maybe her instincts weren't as bad as she thought. Deep down, she also knew that she had been a good wife to him. There was just something in Brian that didn't want to settle down, didn't want to be the man the Lord wanted him to be.

Ronni finished her tea and went to take a shower. She'd shed enough tears over Brian. Enough was enough.

eight

"I think Ronni needs some time to herself," Cole's aunt said as she sipped her tea. "And I don't even know how to approach telling her how sorry I am that my son was unfaithful to her. . .and took us both to the cleaners for that other woman."

"I'm sorry, Aunt Claudia. I don't know what to say to either of you."

She reached across the table and patted his hand. "I know you don't, dear. I can imagine what you are thinking about Brian right about now, and I know you don't want to hurt me by letting it all out."

Cole had to chuckle. His aunt read him well. "I'll try to keep it to myself and the Lord."

"Thank you. I'm thinking some of the same things, you know. I'm very angry at him. At the same time, I'm still mourning the loss of my only son. And I'm wondering what I did so wrong that he turned out the way he did."

"You did nothing wrong, Aunt Claudia. Brian just made a lot of wrong choices. But he was the one who made them. Not you."

"Yes, well. . ." She sighed.

"What do you want Nick to do about all of these charges you didn't make? Miss Marsh should be responsible for them. There's no way you should have to—"

"Cole, you know I don't want to bring charges against

anyone. And it was Brian who is responsible for all of this. He was my son. It's my name that is on that line. I have to pay these debts off. If we can make arrangements for me to pay back the loan without losing the house, then that's what I'd like to do—"

"But Aunt Claudia—"

"We can talk to Nick and see what can be done. But I don't want Ronni to have to be in on the meetings. She's been through enough. I wish she hadn't been there tonight."

"I know. But it wouldn't have been right to hide it from her, either. Tell you what. Let me talk to Nick and try to figure something out."

"Thank you, Cole. Hard as it is, at least we now know the truth."

"I wish it'd all been a bad mistake, Aunt Claudia. But we'll all get through it. I'm not about to leave you to handle it all alone. And you aren't going to lose your home. We're going to figure out a way for you to keep it and to keep the Melrose name respected around here."

"Cole, you are a blessing to me right now. I'm so glad Ronni and I have you to turn to."

He had a feeling that it was highly unlikely that Ronni would be turning to him, much as he wished she would. He was certain that it wasn't going to happen anytime soon. . .if ever.

❧

Cole was out of the house before his aunt or Ronni came downstairs the next morning. He thought it might be easier if Ronni didn't have to see him and remember that he knew about Brian's infidelity. Leaving a note that he was having breakfast downtown, he slipped out and locked the door behind him.

He was determined to find a way to help his aunt. He knew her well, and she wasn't about to sue anyone. If Nick couldn't get this Marsh woman to accept responsibility for some of the debt, then they would have to find some way to pay it all back. Claudia wasn't going to just let her credit and name be ruined. Not without doing all she could to stop it.

The coffee shop was a nice surprise. It served a complete breakfast, and he enjoyed watching and listening to the locals as they came and went. He'd taken time to walk around the older part of town and had been impressed with how so many were working to help it survive. The shops had been given fresh coats of paint. Awnings were mostly new. Some empty shops were for rent, but most were open for business. The people in Magnolia Bay seemed to be fighting hard to revive his favorite place in the world.

But he'd noticed that there were few places to stay in town. There were several motels back up off the interstate and one smaller one on the water's edge. If they were trying to draw tourists back other than for day trips, they needed more lodging. An idea on how he could help his aunt and the town began to form in his mind, but before he could flesh it out fully, the waitress showed up with the breakfast he'd ordered.

With the plate before him, he found he was extra hungry. He buttered the triple layers of pancakes and poured warm maple syrup over the top. They weren't as light and fluffy as his aunt's, but they were good.

He let his idea take hold while he ate, and by the time he finished, he was excited. He wanted to make sure she would keep the home before telling his aunt what he'd come up with, so he called Nick's office and made an appointment for after lunch. Nick told him he'd have more news by then.

When Cole met Nick at his office, he found that the news was about what he expected. Belinda Marsh wasn't making enough to pay back much of anything.

"But she is afraid Claudia will file charges and is willing to put the condo up for sale. She'll give Claudia the proceeds so that she can pay off the bank loan Brian had taken out to buy it," Nick said.

Cole expelled a deep breath. "That is a relief. Can we trust her?"

"I think so. And I'm getting a realtor to handle the sale for her and drawing up papers for her to sign. She says she'll do anything to avoid facing charges."

"You know Aunt Claudia wouldn't let it get that far."

"I do. But Belinda Marsh doesn't."

"Boy, am I glad you are on our side, Nick."

Nick leaned back in his chair and grinned. "Think nothing of it. I'm glad to help Claudia. She's a wonderful woman. Too bad her son was a complete jerk."

"No kidding. Brian and I were never close, but it's hard for me to believe he fell as far from the tree as he did. My uncle and aunt were shining examples of what Christians should be when I was growing up. I know they raised him right."

"How is Ronni?"

Cole shook his head. "I haven't seen her today. I left

before she came downstairs. But she was taking it all pretty hard last night."

"She's been through so much. Meagan told me just the other day that she thought Ronni was beginning to feel like she could finally get on with her life. Now to find out that Brian was unfaithful to her. . ." He blew out a deep breath. "That probably set her back for no telling how long."

Cole had a feeling Nick was right. And that made him angriest of all. "That Brian could do that to her is what I find the most difficult of all to understand."

"I know. I feel the same way."

They sat in silence for a moment before Cole stood to leave. "Thanks again, Nick. Just give me a call if there are more developments."

"I will. I have an appointment with the loan company this afternoon. Once they find out that we have proof Claudia didn't take out that loan, I'm sure they'll back off and give us time to work it all out so they can get their money back."

"I hope so."

"The charges at other places might be a little harder to settle. Belinda says she'll try to pay them a little at a time, but it's unlikely she can make a dent in them anytime soon. I've got my associate Jeff Morrison trying to work things out so that Claudia won't be held responsible, but it may take a little longer."

"Well, get me the total, if you can. I can help Aunt Claudia with some of this. Mostly though, let's just make sure she can keep her home."

"I'm almost positive we can do that."

"I think I have a plan that will help her bring in some income from it and, if need be, pay off some of this stuff. We can't put the money Brian took back in, but if we can keep Aunt Claudia from having to pay out any more, that will be a victory of sorts, don't you think?" Cole asked as he turned to leave.

"I do." Nick followed him to the door. "You know, I can't help but feel just a little sorry for Belinda Marsh. I think Brian was using her, too."

"Wouldn't surprise me a bit. Talk to you later, Nick."

"Later."

❧

Ronni was more than a little relieved that Cole hadn't been downstairs when she came down. It was humiliating for her that both he and Nick knew Brian had been having an affair while she was married to him. But that was the least of her worries right now. It was Claudia she was concerned about.

"Good morning, dear." Claudia interrupted her thoughts. "How are you this morning?"

"I'm. . ." Ronni paused. No. She couldn't lie to Claudia. "I've been better, Mom. How about you? Were you able to sleep?"

"Not a lot. I tossed and turned, trying to figure out why Brian turned out the way he did. I tried to be a good parent and—"

"Oh, Mom! You were a great mother to him. I know you taught him right. And don't think that you are the only one who blames yourself. I still wonder what I did wrong. But I—"

"Ronni, dear!" Claudia interrupted. "You are not to

blame for any of this. I know you were a wonderful wife to Brian. Don't for one minute think I blame you in any way."

The tears in her mother-in-law's voice and eyes had moisture welling up in Ronni's own eyes. She poured herself a cup of coffee and refilled Claudia's cup before sitting down across from her at the table.

"Thank you, Mom. I needed to hear that this morning."

"We can't undo all the bad Brian has done, dear. But neither can we let it destroy us. He was my son, and I loved him with all my heart, just as I know you did. But I can't abide that he hurt you so badly! Or that he intentionally stole from both of us. Now he's gone, and I can't even give him a piece of my mind. I don't know what else to do but hand it over to the Lord. He's got us through so far, Ronni. He'll get us through all of this mess, too."

Ronni sent up a silent prayer that He would. And that she would be able leave it all in His hands. She wanted to rant and rave about the man who'd been her husband, but she couldn't—especially not to his mother and the woman who had brought her to the Lord. Claudia had been through enough pain because of her son, and Ronni wasn't going to bring her any more—not if she could help it.

"Ronni?"

"I'm sorry, Mom. My mind seems to be flitting all over the place today."

"That's understandable. Are you sure you are—"

"I'm all right. Or I will be. We both will be." Ronni didn't know who she was trying to reassure the most, herself or Claudia.

"Yes, we're going to be fine. We have each other and the Lord."

Ronni looked at her watch. "And I'd better get a move on, or I'm going to be late for work. I'll see you this evening. If you need me for anything. . ."

"I know where to find you. Have a good day. I'll update you on any news tonight."

"Okay. Hope it's all good today."

"So do I."

By the time Ronni got to work, she'd found something new to stress about. Did Meagan know about Brian's affair? She was sure Nick didn't ordinarily reveal confidential information, but since she worked for Meagan. . .

No. Nick was a very reputable attorney, and Ronni was sure that he would not discuss Brian's infidelity outside the office. Not even with Meagan. But what did it matter, anyway? Meagan was a wonderful friend, and she needed someone to talk to about all of this.

Ronni pulled up at work and got out of the car, deciding then and there if Meagan didn't know that she was about to. She was just pouring herself a cup of coffee when her friend and employer walked in the door. Ronni peeked around the kitchen door. "Coffee is made."

"Morning, Ronni," Meagan called. "That's just what I need. I was running late today, and I didn't have time to grab a cup before I had to take Tori to school. They are having tests today, and she stayed up late and wasn't the easiest to wake up this morning."

She hurried back to the kitchen and grabbed the cup Ronni held out to her. "Ahh. Wonderful."

"When you have a minute, I'd like to talk to you about something, okay?"

"Sure." Meagan looked at her closely. "What's up? You

need some time off?"

She didn't know. And that made Ronni want to tell her. "No. I just need your ear."

Meagan sat down. "We don't open for another half hour. Sit and tell me all about it."

"I can tell that Nick didn't say anything to you, and my respect for him as an attorney has doubled."

"Say anything to me about what? Are you in need of an attorney, Ronni?"

"No, but Cole hired Nick to help with that financial problem I told you he came to help Claudia with. And well, he found out that it was Brian who put her in such a predicament."

"Oh, Ronni, I'm so sorry. I was hoping it would all be a big mistake."

"I know. So were we all. But it gets worse."

"How?"

"It seems that the charges and loan were due to a woman he was seeing."

"Brian was seeing someone else?"

"He was having an affair."

"You can't be serious. Well, of course you are. You wouldn't make something like this up." Meagan shook her head back and forth, seeming to try and take it all in. "You're sure?"

"Evidently your husband is. He's the one who told us."

"Oh, honey, I am so sorry. I never did like Brian, and I didn't want to tell you that. . .but he—you deserved much better than him."

"Oh, Meagan. I keep wondering how awful a wife I was that he would turn to someone else! I loved him. I tried to be a good wife—"

"Ronni, don't even think like that. The problem wasn't with you. It was Brian. He was the one who was unfaithful to you—not the other way around. And anyone who knows you at all understands that the fault was with him—not you."

"I don't know. I feel that I must have failed him in some way—but I don't know what it was."

"You didn't fail him. *He* failed everyone who ever loved him. I just wish I could make you see that."

"Right now, I'd appreciate it if you would pray for me to get over this anger I'm filled with. Not only that he betrayed me—I knew our marriage wasn't what it should have been, and I hope one day I figure out what I did wrong there—but that he could have used his mother and put her in such a financial bind. How could he have done that to Claudia?"

"I will pray for you, Ronni; but I think the Lord understands your anger, and I'm certain He will help you deal with it. I'm quite sure He's not happy about what Brian did, either. And while I'm at it, I'm also going to pray that He shows you the truth. The only mistake you made was to fall in love with the wrong man.

⚜

By the time Cole got back to his aunt's that afternoon, his idea on how best to help her was pretty well formed. He was glad to see that she was home when he got there and hoped that she liked his plan.

She was in the kitchen, kneading a large mass of dough rather vigorously, from what he could see. As she pounded a fist into the middle of it, he wondered if she might be taking out her anger with Brian on the dough.

"That's sure to be a great loaf of bread from the way you are manhandling it."

"Oh!" She whirled around, a floured hand pressed to her heart. "Cole! I didn't hear you drive up. You scared me."

He hurried over, put his arms around her, and led her to a chair. "I'm so sorry, Aunt Claudia. Are you all right?"

She took a deep breath and chuckled before answering him. "I'm okay. I was just lost in my thoughts, I guess." She got up and went back to her bread. "I'd better get this dough in the loaf pans; I've probably kneaded it long enough."

Cole got a soft drink out of the refrigerator and leaned against the kitchen counter, watching her shape the loaves and place them in the pans. She covered them with a dishcloth and put them at the back of the stove to rise. She washed her hands and dried them, then poured herself a glass of iced tea. "Come sit with me awhile."

He joined her at the table, glad to be able to tell her the newest developments. "I talked to Nick earlier today, and he just gave me another call on my way here. I think I have some good news for you."

"Oh, I hope so. I sure could use some." She took a sip of tea and looked at him expectantly.

"Here is what we have. Nick has been in touch with the loan officer at the national company Brian did business with and with Belinda Marsh. The lender has agreed to wait until she can sell the condo and get the money to you so that you can pay off the home-equity loan."

"Oh, Cole. Has she agreed to this?"

"Yes, she has. Eagerly from what Nick told me. She doesn't know that you would probably lose your house rather than take her to court, Aunt Claudia. And that's a good thing. She's willing to do whatever it takes to stay out of court."

"And he got the lender to hold off on foreclosing on this property?"

Cole nodded. "Nick explained that if he doesn't want a lot of bad publicity in this part of the country and a fight in court about how they didn't do a thorough background check—like they should have when Brian took out that loan in your name—they might want to reconsider pressing you right now."

Claudia started chuckling. It was good to hear his aunt laugh again. "Oh, Cole, this is such wonderful news!"

"It is. But the things charged to your account—Miss Marsh says she will try to pay them back, but Nick says she's not making that kind of money. So I'm going to pay those charges for you, if you will let me, Aunt Claudia."

"No, Cole. I can't let you do that—"

"Aunt Claudia, for years you welcomed me into this home and loved me and cared for me. You've been like a mother to me. Please let me do this for you."

"I. . .oh, Cole."

"Please. And I have another idea about how you can get back on your feet and help Magnolia Bay at the same time."

"You do?"

"Yes. You may not like it, though. And that's all right. But I think you might."

"Well, lay it out for me, then."

"Okay. I've been touring Magnolia Bay, and I am so impressed by the way Bay Drive is being revitalized and the way the whole downtown area is trying to make a comeback. I think your committee is doing a wonderful job of encouraging new businesses to come in and old ones to start back up. But have you noticed that the town is badly lacking in overnight accommodations?"

"We have had many discussions on the subject. But no clear-cut answers. There are a couple of nice motels up on the interstate, but with all the competition from the casino's hotels, we haven't had any success in trying to get any of the chains to build down here on the bay. We're hoping that someone will decide to put up a small, privately run hotel someday."

"You know, Melrose Manor is very large." Cole then kept silent, waiting for his aunt to make the connection.

It didn't take long. "What are you saying? I should turn it into a hotel?"

"No. Not a hotel, exactly—maybe a large bed-and-breakfast or an inn?"

She sat silently, tapping her fingertips together.

He waited for her to refuse outright. This was her home, after all. It would have to be difficult to think about turning it into a business venture.

"I don't know. Do you think we could do it?" There was a sparkle in her eyes as she continued. "We'd have to do some remodeling. . .add some bathrooms on, wouldn't we?"

"Yes, it would require making changes. And everything would be a mess for a while." Cole was relieved that she hadn't turned down the idea outright. She seemed to be thinking it over. . .and if he was reading her right, she seemed to like it.

"Do you really think it could be done?"

"Aunt Claudia, I'm an architect. Do you think I would suggest it if it couldn't be?"

"Oh, Cole, much as I like the idea—and I do—this is a very big place, and it can get awfully lonely at times. I love having people around and entertaining. It's a wonderful suggestion, and I don't know why I never thought of it. But you know what my financial situation is. It would take a lot of money, and I don't think I can afford to do it, Cole. I really don't want to go to the bank for it. . .not even my own. Not that they would be eager to lend me any money after the mess Brian put me in."

"I can put up the money, if you'll let me. It's something I'd love to do for you, Aunt Claudia." He could tell she really did like the idea, and he wanted to make it happen for her.

But she began shaking her head even as she got up from the table and went to refill her tea glass. "I can't let you do that, dear. It could take years to make it back and—"

"Okay, how about if you make me a partner in the business?"

She paused, the tea pitcher in her hand. "A partner?"

Cole had a feeling he'd caught her attention. "Yes. A small one, though. Just enough for you not to feel badly about letting me help. And keep in mind that an inn would surely fill a need here in Magnolia Bay. Just think about it, will you?"

"I'll think about it." She poured her tea and set the pitcher down. "I like the idea. But I'd want Ronni in on the decision making."

"I understand, and she should be."

"And you are confident it can be done?"

"I'm sure," Cole said, understanding her need for reassurance. "I've been drawing up plans in my mind all day. I'd like to get some of it down on paper so you can see what I'm talking about. With three stories to this house, you have plenty of room to have family quarters and your guest quarters. You could easily have six guest rooms, maybe more."

"What about bathrooms? I know a lot of B&Bs have shared bathrooms, but I'd like to offer private ones."

"Your rooms are plenty large enough so that shouldn't be a problem. The hard part will be making sure we don't take away from the historical value of the home." He grinned at her. "Fortunately for us, I know how to do that."

"This would mean not only giving your money but your time, too. Cole, you have a business in Texas to run—"

"I can do both, Aunt Claudia. Just think about it, okay?"

nine

"Think about what?" Ronni asked as she entered the kitchen and found Claudia and Cole in deep conversation. Ordinarily, she wouldn't have been so rude as to interrupt them, but with the mess Brian had left them in, she wanted to know all she could about what was going on. After all, Cole knew things about her and Brian that she hadn't even wanted to know.

"Oh, Ronni, I'm glad you are home!" Claudia exclaimed. "Cole has news, and he's come up with an idea to help us out."

"Oh?"

"Yes, but I need to start supper and—"

"I'll help. Tell me what you need me to do."

Claudia actually looked excited. There was a sparkle in her eyes that Ronni hadn't seen in days.

Claudia got up from the table and started toward the stove. "I'm making stew and bread. I have everything prepared. I just need to brown the meat and add everything else in. It won't take but a minute."

"Mom, go sit down and let me do this tonight. You and Cole can fill me in on what's been happening while I get the stew going." She was surprised when Claudia did as she suggested.

While Ronni browned the stew meat in the dutch oven Claudia liked to use, they filled her in on everything. By the time they finished telling her about Belinda Marsh and how Nick had handled everything, Ronni began to relax. Nick Chambers was a very good lawyer. It looked like Claudia would be able to keep the house after all.

"Oh, Mom, that is wonderful news," Ronni said as she added potatoes, carrots, and onions to the meat. "Nick told us he thought she'd do all she could to keep from having to go to jail. I'm so glad he was right."

"So am I. But that's not all the good news today. Cole has come up with a brilliant idea for me to be able to keep up the house and grounds and help Magnolia Bay all at the same time."

"Oh?"

"Come sit down with us, and I'll let him explain it all."

Ronni turned the burner down and washed her hands before making herself a glass of tea and joining them at the kitchen table. They were both grinning from ear to ear. "It must be something good from the expressions on your faces. Okay. Fill me in."

"Cole thinks we could turn Melrose Manor into an inn."

"An inn—as in a hotel or a bed-and-breakfast?"

Claudia was nodding vigorously. "Yes. A kind of little hotel or a big B&B. I guess we'd need to discuss how many meals to serve and—"

"You will serve meals, too?"

"Oh, dear. I didn't mean to just dump all of this in your lap, Ronni. What I really want is your opinion about it all."

"Mom, this is your home. What you choose to do with it is up to you. But what about all the start-up costs involved?"

"I'm going to put up that money for Aunt Claudia," Cole informed her.

"Only if he lets me make him a partner in the business," Claudia quickly added.

"A very small partner," Cole insisted. "It was the only way I could get her to agree to let me help her."

"I see." Only Ronni wasn't sure she did. All she knew at this point was that more changes were on the way.

"Well, what do you think?" Claudia asked. "It's a way for me to be able to get out of the mess Brian left me in. And almost as good, it's a way for me to help Magnolia Bay. The town really does need more overnight accommodations."

She seemed so happy and excited. Ronni wasn't about to burst her bubble. If Claudia wanted to turn her home into an inn, then who was she to object? "If that's what you want to do, Mom, I think you should go for it."

"Really?"

"Absolutely."

"Cole is going to draw up the blueprints for some of the changes that will need to be made. Should the family quarters be on the second or third floor?"

"I can draw up two different plans showing them in both places, so that you can see what you think, Aunt Claudia."

"That would be wonderful. Then we could see the layout of the rooms and—should we use the downstairs rooms as public ones or reserve them for our private use?"

"Why don't you let Cole draw up those plans and then decide, Mom?" Ronni asked. It was truly wonderful to see her so enthused and happy.

"Yes, that will be best. But, oh, the more I think of it all, the better I like the idea. Do you think we should keep the name Melrose Manor or change it?"

"Mom, you and Cole can decide that. I'm going to finish

dinner while you two make these decisions."

"Ronni, this is your home, too. And you will inherit it one day, just as Brian would have. I need your input."

"I don't feel I should be—"

"Ronni, dear, I really need your help. If you aren't in on this from the beginning, I don't think I want any part of it."

"But, Mom—"

"She really means it, Ronni. We both need your input in this venture. Won't you please help us?"

"Please, Ronni. I want to do this, but I don't think I have the courage to if you aren't a part of it all." Claudia looked like she was about to cry.

She'd certainly had enough sorrow this week. Ronni couldn't bring her more. She got up and went around the table to hug Claudia. "All right, Mom. If this is what you really want to do, then I'll help all I can. You know that."

Claudia returned the hug, the smile back on her face. "Thank you, dear. We really do need your input."

Ronni was doubtful about that, but she'd be as supportive as possible. "Well, let's have supper, and then we can discuss this to your heart's content."

❧

By the time Ronni got to her room that night, her mind was whirling with all the ideas Claudia and Cole had thrown out. As she showered and got ready for bed, she had to admit that it was hard not to get excited about this inn thing.

At first she was a little concerned that Claudia had jumped on it as a diversion from the pain of learning Brian had put her in such financial jeopardy. But as the evening wore on, she could tell Claudia really liked the idea of turning her home into a nice place for people to stay. She did love people and entertaining, although she hadn't done much of that since Brian's death. But Ronni could remember some of the dinner parties Claudia would have for friends from church and the city council, and Claudia had always been able to make everyone feel comfortable and at home. She would be a wonderful innkeeper.

But all of the renovations meant that Cole would be around more. It appeared he was increasingly involving himself in their lives whether she wanted him to or not. Obviously, Claudia was happy about it. But Ronni wasn't sure how she felt about him being around all that often. She was still uncomfortable around him, and she didn't know whether it was because she was way too attracted to him for her own peace of mind or if it was because he'd been a witness to her most humiliating moment—finding out that her husband had been unfaithful to her.

Part of Ronni resented that Claudia needed his help now, but she was impressed with Cole's good heart. He truly wanted to help Claudia, and he could afford to do it. Claudia needed more help than Ronni was able to give right now, and she prayed that the Lord would help her to keep that in mind. Cole's idea did seem to be a good plan, and she needed to remember how excited her mother-in-law was about it.

All in all, this day was an improvement on the one before. She felt much better after her talk with Meagan. She was still very angry, but she felt that was justified. Brian had made so many wrong choices, and he'd hurt her and Claudia deeply. . .and no telling how many more people. The choices Brian had made were his choices, and

Ronni was coming to realize that nothing she could have said or done would have made a difference to him. She didn't need to be wasting time wondering what she could have done to change things. No, she needed to get on with her life and feel the joy she had begun to experience only a few weeks ago.

She walked out onto the balcony and breathed in the fresh night air. Hearing a rustling noise below, she looked down just in time to see Cole take off down the walking trail. For a moment, she wanted to call out to him to wait for her, but she resisted the urge. She shouldn't even be thinking about Cole. She'd promised herself long ago that she was not going to put herself in a position of getting hurt again. Right now, that meant tamping down any growing attraction she might be feeling for Cole. Any. Even the least little bit.

She went back inside and almost dove into bed. After plumping up her pillow, she turned out the bedside light and sent up an added prayer that the Lord would keep her from falling for the man. She just couldn't put her heart on the line again.

❧

Cole slipped out the door and headed for the walking trail. He was way too keyed up to sleep after all the planning they'd been doing. His aunt really seemed excited about turning the manor into an inn, and he couldn't wait to get started on the changes they would need to make.

He wasn't really sure what Ronni thought about it all, but his respect for her had climbed even higher when she gave Claudia her unconditional support. She'd been through so much in the last few days. What must it feel like to find out that one's mate hadn't been faithful?

He didn't know and never wanted to find out. Cole began to jog. He sure wished Brian were here right now. He'd like nothing better than to teach him a thing or two about how to treat the people who loved him. Feeling the disgust and anger build against his cousin for what he'd put Aunt Claudia and Ronni through, Cole picked up speed and began to run.

As a Christian, he knew he should be feeling sorry for the man instead of wishing he were here so he could deck him. But it wasn't easy to do. He prayed that the Lord would calm him down. Brian wasn't here, anyway, and there was nothing one could do to him now. He'd done it all to himself.

Brian could have had such a wonderful life with Ronni. Instead he chose to ruin that life. Perhaps, had he lived, he might have brought more sorrow to those he loved, although Cole found it hard to think in what way. He just hoped that his aunt and Ronni could get past the hurt and pain they were both feeling and get on with their lives.

When he got to the point that overlooked the bay, Cole stopped and looked heavenward.

"Dear Lord, please help Ronni and Aunt Claudia to get past this latest setback. Please ease the pain Ronni must feel at learning Brian was unfaithful to her—and the turmoil of emotions she must be experiencing because of it. I pray if this idea I've given Aunt Claudia is Your will that it will all come together in the way You would have it. And, Father, please let Ronni realize what a special person she is. I think she may doubt that right now. She's embarrassed because Claudia and Nick and I know just how badly Brian treated her. Please take that away from her. In Jesus' name, amen."

It was a beautiful night. Spring was just around the corner, and everything seemed on the verge of blooming or coming to life. He hoped it would be that way for Ronni. And he had a feeling it wasn't just for her sake but possibly for his own.

He had to admit that he looked forward to having a reason to spend more time in Magnolia Bay. And he especially liked the opportunity that offered his getting to know Ronni better.

She was a special lady. He certainly didn't know any others who would be as caring of a mother-in-law. Yet he could see that she and Claudia had grown close from all they'd gone through together.

Cole turned to go back to the house. Ideas were still coming to him fast and furious on how best to turn his aunt's home into an inn that would still be home to her. He couldn't wait to get started on those plans. He began to run. He had to get his ideas written down on paper so that he didn't lose any of them.

☙

After church the next day, they were all asked to go out to eat at the Seaside Surf and Turf with Nick and Meagan; Nick's grandmother, Hattie; and his teenage sister, Tori. Ronni was a little afraid the conversation would turn to Brian, but by the time they got to the main course, she realized that she should have known better. None of these people were going to bring up a subject that would embarrass her and Claudia.

Instead, the conversation revolved around the possible

renovation of the manor. Meagan's late grandmother and Claudia had been on the revitalization committee for Magnolia Bay, and it was apparent Claudia wanted to see what Meagan thought her grandmother's opinion of the idea would have been. "You're really thinking of turning your home into an inn, Miss Claudia?" Meagan asked once Claudia had told them of Cole's idea.

"I think so. I am really excited about his suggestions. Not only will it help me out of the bind Brian left me in," Claudia said, as if everyone at the table knew what he'd done, "but it will also give me a chance to help Magnolia Bay with much-needed accommodations."

"Well, we could certainly use a few more rooms in this town; that's for sure," Hattie Chambers said.

"I certainly like the idea," Claudia assured them. "It will mean a lot of mess for a while and some changes in our family space, but Ronni and I have way too much of that anyway, don't we, dear?"

"Yes, we do," Ronni agreed. She had a feeling that her mother-in-law was seeking her reassurance once more. "Some rooms we never go into except to air out and clean."

"Cole has already been working on plans for the renovations. I can't wait to see them," Claudia told them.

"I've seen many of Cole's designs in Dallas," Meagan said. "I'm sure he will do an exceptional job of keeping it your home while turning it into a place people will be making reservations for long in advance."

"You're that good, are you?" Nick grinned.

"Well—"

"He's as good an architect as you are an attorney, love," Meagan interrupted with a grin.

Nick smiled at his wife. "Oh. Well then, of course, he's *that good.*"

"Of course I am," Cole agreed.

Everyone at the table laughed at Nick and Cole's banter, and Ronni felt better about the changes the manor was about to undergo. Evidently, Cole knew what he was doing and was very good at it. She had to admit to herself that she was looking forward to seeing what he came up with.

"I thought maybe we could also hold weddings and showers, birthday parties, and the like on the grounds," Claudia suggested. "Do you think that's a good idea?"

"Oh, I like that," Ronni said.

"I could hire a caterer to help with the food, and I'd use the local florists for the arrangements. We'd have to have a small housekeeping staff, too," Claudia added.

"That is a truly wonderful idea, Miss Claudia," Meagan said. "My grams would love it! And you'd be hiring people from the area. That would help Magnolia Bay even more than the extra rooms."

"Yes, that's what I thought." Claudia nodded her head. "The more I think about it, the better it gets."

"I am so glad you are so enthused about this, Mom. It's really good to see you excited about this idea," Ronni said honestly, relieved that her worries about her mother-in-law overdoing things had just been taken care of. And it really was wonderful to see her so animated and happy. Obviously, Claudia had been doing a lot of thinking about it all.

Ronni glanced over at Cole and found him studying her. He smiled and winked at her. Suddenly her pulse took off at triple speed, and she could feel the color rise in her face as she forced herself to look away. She wasn't sure what expression she saw in his eyes, but whatever it was had her heart beating so hard she could almost hear it.

ten

Claudia's ideas didn't stop at Sunday dinner. For the next few days, she came up with at least two or three a day while Cole worked on the plans he was drawing up. All Ronni knew about it was that he was using some kind of CAD program on his computer and he promised Claudia that she would be able to see his plans in 3-D once he was through with them.

"The reception area will be in the foyer. I think that will work really well since it's so large. And there is so much furniture in the house and the attic that we should be able to rotate pieces so returning guests will see something new each time they come."

Claudia and Ronni were putting the finishing touches on dinner when Cole came in from the study, a huge grin on his face. "I think it's ready for you two ladies' approval."

"You're finished?" Claudia asked excitedly.

"I believe so. . .except for any last-minute changes you might add."

Claudia's numerous changes had become a running joke in the last few days.

"Well, hard as it's going to be, I think we should wait until after supper so we can go over the plans at our leisure."

"Sounds good to me." Cole rotated his head from side to side and rubbed the back of his neck.

Ronni had been told she gave great neck massages and

had the urge to ask him if he needed a neck and shoulder rub, but the thought of being that close to him had her pulse racing so she kept her offer to herself. All she said was, "I'm sure Cole could use a break from that computer for a while."

"A break won't hurt." He sniffed appreciatively. "Especially if it includes eating dinner. It sure smells good in here."

"Roast chicken and vegetables. It will be on the table in just a few minutes."

"Well, let me at least help set the table," he said, taking the silverware from Ronni.

A bolt of electricity shot up her arm at the brush of their fingers. Ronni quickly turned to fill glasses from the ice maker, hoping Cole couldn't tell how flustered she felt. Aggravated with herself for feeling anything at all, she poured the tea and turned back to find Cole right behind her, his hand out to take one of the glasses from her. She startled in surprise, sloshing some of the tea from one glass.

"I'm sorry, Ronni. I thought you knew I was here."

"It's okay. I'm just klutzy today, I guess," Ronni said as she mopped up the floor. She wasn't about to tell him that normally she wasn't, but around him, she found herself more than a little clumsy.

"You're always graceful. I just surprised you, that's all." He picked up one of the glasses and the pitcher and took them to the table while Ronni followed with the other two glasses.

Claudia joined them at the table with the platter of chicken and roasted potatoes, carrots, and onions. After

Cole said the blessing, Ronni looked up to find Claudia looking from her to Cole and back again as they fixed their plates. "I can't tell you two how much it means to me to have you with me. I thank the Lord for you both each day."

"We're thankful for you, too, Mom." Ronni didn't even want to think of how hard the past year would have been without Claudia's support and love.

"I know. And that's what makes it even more special to have you here. I am so excited about this new venture. I feel as though a new chapter has started in my life, and I am thrilled and scared all at the same time. If I didn't have your support, I don't think I'd have the courage to think about turning this place into an inn."

"Oh, Aunt Claudia, you have more courage than nearly anyone I know. But if having us here makes all of this easier on you, I'm glad. And I'm anxious to see what you think of the plans."

"I can hardly wait to look at them." Claudia served herself. "Whatever you've come up with, I know that it will be wonderful."

"Well, reserve judgment until you see them. I've got two versions: One is with the family living quarters on the third floor, and the other is with them on the second."

"Which plan do you think will work best?" Ronni asked, caught up in the planning in spite of herself.

"I'll tell you after you've looked at them. It's actually up to you and Aunt Claudia as it will affect you two the most. But I think you're going to be surprised at how well this house lends itself to the changes."

They didn't linger over dinner, in anticipation of seeing the plans. Cole helped clear the table and then went to the study to set up the computer while Ronni rinsed and put the dishes in the dishwasher and Claudia wiped down the table and countertops. She also put on a pot of decaffeinated coffee and brought out a plate of cookies for later.

By the time they headed for the study, Ronni didn't know who was the most anxious about seeing the plans, she or Claudia. Cole was coming out of the room just as they were about to enter, his laptop in hand.

"I think it might be easier if I set this up at the kitchen table. You'll both be able to see more easily from there." So back they went and waited until he had it all set up again.

He handed them both several printed pages as the program was coming up, and Ronni was surprised at the detailed planning. As Cole began to point out the changes on the computer screen, they could see the same plans in 3-D.

"The rooms upstairs are arranged so that it was easy to bring in the existing shared bathroom of two adjoining rooms into one, and then, by cutting a few feet from each side of two adjoining rooms, to put a bathroom into the other one. There will be a shower, lavatory, and toilet in each of those rooms, with the remaining rooms on each side of the hall—yours and Ronni's—having the larger bathrooms as they do now. We'll update them somewhat with whirlpool baths in each. You could charge a little more for those rooms, Aunt Claudia."

"Oh, Cole, these plans are wonderful!"

And they were. Ronni was very impressed by what he'd done. In fact the rooms looked little different than they did now, except that the sitting areas were a little smaller.

"I love the way you've kept the six rooms on the second

floor intact with a fireplace in each one," Claudia said.

"We could make the rooms smaller yet and give you another room on each side of the hall, but—"

"Oh no," Claudia interrupted. "I love the way you've done this. And I want the rooms to be a nice size."

Ronni breathed a sigh of relief. She'd hate to see the rooms chopped up. She liked the way Cole had taken care to change as little as possible while adding a private bathroom to each one.

Cole switched plans, showing the living quarters on the third floor. His talent was truly apparent. He'd made a large living-dining combination, with a fireplace in each section, and a modern galley kitchen that would be easy to work in. He'd included four bedrooms, two with their own bath and two sharing a bath. It was both cozy and elegant.

"Oh, how lovely this will be," Claudia breathed.

"Yes, it is really very nice," Ronni added as she looked the plans over carefully. She'd never dreamed he would be able to make truly livable and comfortable family quarters that would feel like home. But she could see how easy it would be to live in the space he'd envisioned.

"Now, I can show you the plan switched around, so that you can decide where you'd like the family quarters."

That he'd given these plans a lot of thought was obvious from the detail present in each rendering. He'd included an elevator for both plans, explaining that they had to adhere to ADA regulations and that it would also add to the marketability of the inn, but Ronni was pleased for a completely different reason. Claudia would be getting older through the years, and climbing those stairs would most likely become hard for her. . .especially if the private living quarters were on the third floor. But she really liked the first plans better and hoped that Claudia did, too.

"You have done a magnificent job with these plans, Cole. I do believe that I like the first ones best, though," Claudia said. She chuckled and shook her head. "I'm not so sure I would if you hadn't added that elevator, but with it, I think I'd like being on the third floor. I want my guests to be comfortable, but I want the family to be able to take in the exquisite views from the third floor. It will be wonderful to really use all the space in this home, again. . .even if it won't be only for the family use. Back when the Melrose family was so large and everyone came for the summer from all over, I'm sure this house could be bursting at the seams. But it's been years since it has been used in that way. I can't wait to have it full of people once more."

Claudia seemed to be lost in thought for a moment, and Ronni had a feeling she was thinking of Brian and the dreams she'd had of having her grandchildren fill the old home with laughter and fun. But that dream died with her son, and now Cole had come up with an idea that would fill this house with life for Claudia once more. She glanced over at him and found his gaze on her.

"What do you think, Ronni?" he asked.

"I think Mom is right. The first plans are the ones I would choose. Having the family quarters on the third floor will give us more privacy, too."

"And that might be a welcome relief after dealing with guests all day," Claudia added.

"Mom, are you sure this is what you want to do?"

"I am. But much as I am excited about all of this, I want you both to know that I understand that it's not going to be easy. There will be days when I'll probably wonder if I've lost my mind in making this decision. But I do believe that it is something I will love doing. And it will be my contribution to helping this town. For all of that, I think a bad day now and then will be a small price to pay for a new adventure. As long as I have the support of you two, I'm ready to get started."

"You know you do," Ronni said, putting an arm around her shoulders.

"Then we'll get going as soon as possible," Cole said, turning off the computer. "You two can go over these plans for the next several days and see if there is anything you want to add. After that, it won't be so easy to change things, okay?"

"I think you've covered about everything I wanted. . .and even some things I hadn't thought of. Thank you, dear." Claudia got up and kissed him on the cheek before going to get the cookie plate and bring it to the table.

Ronni poured the coffee, wishing she could thank Cole in a similar manner. He'd somehow brought a zest for living back into Claudia's life, and for that, she would be ever thankful.

❧

Cole let himself out of the kitchen long after his aunt and Ronni had gone upstairs. He'd thought that once his aunt had approved of the plans, he would be able to sleep like a baby. But he found his thoughts were too full of Ronni to sleep.

He didn't bother with walking tonight but started out at a jog on the path he was getting to know very well. He hadn't realized how much Ronni's acceptance of the plans had meant to him until he saw her reaction to them. She liked his ideas for the renovation. He could see it in her eyes.

Cole had been sure his aunt would like them—after all, she'd been giving him input for the past several days, and she was truly excited about turning Melrose Manor into an inn. He wasn't so sure about Ronni—how she really felt about everything. All he knew was that she was consistently supportive of his aunt, and that meant more to him with each passing day. She didn't have to be so encouraging to Aunt Claudia. But she was, and her approval of the changes meant almost more to him than his aunt's did.

He was frankly amazed at her grace under such trying circumstances. To have been left with nothing when Brian died and then to find out that he'd dealt her another blow almost a year later—Cole didn't think he could have shown the grace and perseverance that Ronni had. How could his cousin not have appreciated what he had?

Were she his wife, Cole couldn't imagine being unfaithful to her. He would look forward to coming home to her each day, to sharing life with her. No, he'd never understand his cousin. Not even if he lived to be a hundred years old.

⋆

Magnolia Bay being as small as it was, word got out quickly that the Melroses were taking bids on the work to be done, and by the end of the week, they had already received several good ones. Cole figured that they'd be able to hire a contractor to do the renovations very soon.

Nick was handling all the legalities of their new partnership and getting the new business started, and when he came out to the house to have some papers signed, he had more good news. Belinda Marsh had already sold the condo. Housing was at a premium along the Gulf Coast, and as the condo was in Biloxi, it went for a good price.

"We have enough money to pay off the bank and the charges on your accounts, Miss Claudia," he said when he came out to give them the news.

"Oh, Nick. What a relief that is! My home will be free and clear as we start this business venture."

"I wish we could have recovered all the money Brian took out of your accounts, but we can't prove Miss Marsh got any of that money, and—"

Claudia shook her head. "It was Brian who took that money. I have my home again and can pay off those other charges. I may not have as much as I once did, but I'm thrilled that I'll be able to keep the Melrose home and have a way of maintaining it. Whatever extra money that woman has from the sale, she can keep. Maybe it will help her start a new life. I will pray she's learned from this experience."

"I hope so, too," Ronni said quietly.

"I've had one of my associates, Jeff Morrison, working with her. He thinks she has learned something," Nick said. "He thinks that she was a victim, too. She claims she didn't know Brian was married."

Cole felt uncomfortable being in the same room while they were discussing this topic. "I've got to make some phone calls. I'll let you all decide what needs to be done concerning the Marsh woman—"

"You don't have to leave, Cole." Ronni seemed to be reading his mind. "It's not as if you don't know what is going on or what Brian did."

"I know. I just thought you might feel more comfortable if I wasn't in the room."

Her smile was brief, but it was there for a moment. "I'd feel more comfortable if I could leave the room. As it stands, I do hope she didn't know he was married."

"We don't have to talk about it anymore at all, dear," Claudia said. "We can pray that Belinda Marsh changes her ways, but we don't have to discuss her ever again as far as I'm concerned. Ronni has had enough heartache."

No kidding, Cole thought. *Enough for a lifetime.*

"This mess is settled as far as I am concerned," his aunt continued. "The banker will be repaid, and the charges to my accounts cleared up. With the Lord's help, we can get on with our lives."

Ronni was quiet for a moment, and Cole wondered what she was thinking. He silently prayed that she would be able to put her past with Brian to rest and begin to get on with the rest of her life.

eleven

Too restless to turn in that night, Ronni felt the need to go for a walk before she went to bed. She put on her walking shoes, ran downstairs, and let herself out the back door. The nights were getting warmer, as were the days. February had slipped into March, and she still hadn't planted anything. She told herself she'd stop at the nursery after work the next day and pick up some bedding plants.

She started down the walking trail, wondering when work on the renovations would start and what company would be doing the work. She'd heard Cole and Claudia discussing the different bids they'd received but had left the deciding up to the two of them. She figured things would be a mess for several months and did dread that, but after going over Cole's plans, she was sure it would be worth it. He was very gifted.

Her mind couldn't settle on one thought for more than a few minutes as she fought hard to try to avoid thinking about Belinda Marsh and Brian. She didn't want to think about them—not individually and certainly not together. Yet she couldn't help but be curious as to what kind of woman Belinda Marsh was. Ronni knew that finding out wouldn't bring Brian back, wouldn't make their marriage any better, and wouldn't really give her any answers as to why he'd been unfaithful to her. He was the only one who could give her the answers she needed, and he was gone.

Ronni began to walk faster. Maybe the fresh air would help clear her mind. She knew she didn't have to worry about having to discuss it all with Claudia, not only because her mother-in-law had said they never needed to discuss Brian's involvement with the Marsh woman again, but because they had always avoided talking about him any more than was absolutely necessary.

She hadn't wanted to bring her mother-in-law more pain by telling her how badly Brian had treated her in those last months when things had gotten so bad. And she was sure Claudia had felt the same way. They both knew he had a problem with gambling and drinking—and there had been no need to rehash all of that. The only thing they hadn't been aware of was his affair with Belinda Marsh. Yet Jeff supposedly thought Belinda had been lied to, too. Jeff had become a good friend of hers in the last year, and she trusted his judgment. . .yet. . .no. There wasn't any reason to go over any of that. Brian was gone. Ronni couldn't and wouldn't let thoughts of him and this Marsh woman bring her more pain.

Spring was in the air. She desperately needed to feel like she had begun to weeks ago. . .as if she were alive again and looking toward the future instead of the past. Yet the future sometimes seemed quite lonely and empty. Ronni picked up speed, trying to shake off the forlornness she'd been fighting all evening.

It was a quiet night, and she thought she heard footsteps. But when Ronni glanced behind her, she could see the lights from the house and no one on the path. She must be imagining things. She rounded a bend in the trail, and her heart plummeted to her stomach before it seemed to stop beating. Someone was coming toward her. Ronni froze, and her pulse began to pound in her ears. She wanted to scream, but no sound would come out. Looking from side to side, she was unsure of where to go. She turned—

"Ronni, wait! It's me, Cole. Don't be afraid," his voice called, strong and reassuring as he jogged toward her.

She was shaking so hard she could barely stand when he reached her. She placed her hand over her heart in an effort to calm its frantic beating.

"Ronni, are you all right?" Cole placed a hand on her arm.

She nodded as she forced herself to take deep gulps of air, trying to get her breathing under control.

"I'm so sorry I frightened you. I've been jogging nearly every night I've been here. I didn't know you were out here."

"I. . ." She inhaled and exhaled. "I'm. . .okay."

"Are you sure?"

"I. . .will. . .be," she managed to get out. A nervous giggle escaped, and then a small sob seemed to come from nowhere.

"You're trembling," Cole said, pulling her into his arms. "Ronni, I am so sorry."

"Not. . .your. . .fault." She didn't know why she was crying now—or why she was letting herself settle into the comfort of Cole's embrace.

"It will be all right, Ronni." His hand rubbed her back. "Cry it out."

"I. . .don't even know. . .what I'm crying for."

"You've had a lot to deal with. Maybe it's just delayed reaction to it all. Brian—"

"I'm sorry. I'm getting your shirt all wet," Ronni said,

pulling out of Cole's arms. Brian was the last person she wanted to talk about. She had to change the subject. "I'm all right now. Let's go back to the house."

Cole looked like he wanted to say more, but she turned and started back up the trail. She managed a small chuckle. "I think I've had enough fresh air for one night."

"It is a beautiful night, though, isn't it? I jog most nights around this time. If you want to join me anytime, I'd like the company."

"Thanks, Cole." She didn't know what to say next. She thought she would love sharing the walking trail with him, but that was a problem in itself. She couldn't let herself like it too much.

"I think we are going to award the contract to Jim Seymour's company. I like working with local contractors, and I'm glad his bid was the best one."

Ronni was relieved that he'd changed the subject. "He's a member of our church. I've heard good things about his company."

"He also is able to start up quickly. That was a big plus. But I have to go to Texas for a few days. I've been trying to keep up with everything online, but one of my projects needs my attention. I'll check in with you and Aunt Claudia each night, but if there is anything you think needs my attention quickly, you still have my phone numbers, right?"

"I do." They were tucked inside her personal address book on the desk in her room.

"Good. Don't hesitate to call if you need to talk to me about anything, okay?"

"Okay." Ronni couldn't imagine picking up the phone and dialing his number just because she might want to hear his voice, but she didn't utter the thought.

Cole locked the back door after they went inside. "I think I'll watch the late news before I go up."

"Okay. I. . .I'm sorry I got mascara on your shirt."

"Oh? Did you?" He looked down at the brown smudge she'd left on his old shirt. "Not a problem."

"If you leave it in the laundry room, I'll treat it and wash it for you."

"Don't worry about it, Ronni. It's an old shirt."

"Well—night, then." She started up the stairs.

"Night. See you tomorrow."

≈

Cole watched Ronni leave the room, sending up a silent prayer that she was all right. He felt horrible that he'd frightened her out on the trail. She'd been shaking so hard that all he could think to do was hold her until she stopped.

She had fit into his arms perfectly, and he hadn't wanted to let her go. But of course, he had. He knew he was falling in love with her but didn't think she would welcome that news. Cole had a feeling she didn't trust him or any other man right now.

By the time, later in the week, when he left for Texas, he wondered if Ronni would ever see him as anything but Claudia's nephew or Brian's cousin. She appeared comfortable enough when another person was around— when they shared a meal with Claudia or were at church— but if they were alone in a room, she seemed ill at ease and always managed to find something that needed attention in another room.

He wanted to tell her his thoughts about what Brian had

done, but when he tried to bring up his cousin's name in any way, she changed the subject or suddenly remembered something that she had to do. It was as if she put up a wall of some kind, and he didn't know how to break it down or get around it. But he sure wanted to. Badly.

He found himself hurrying downstairs of a morning so he could see her before she went to work, and at night, he waited outside for ten or fifteen minutes past the usual time, hoping she would take him up on his offer to keep him company on his jogs. She never did.

He kept himself busy while he was in Dallas, but he found his thoughts were on Magnolia Bay and Ronni most of the time. He missed her and couldn't wait to get back to Mississippi. He'd even begun to think about settling down there. It wasn't likely he'd ever get Ronni to notice him in the way he wanted her to—not with him living in Dallas and her in Magnolia Bay.

On Thursday, after he finished packing his bag for the trip back to Magnolia Bay the next day, he punched in his aunt's phone number on his cordless phone and waited for her to pick up. His heartbeat sped up when Ronni answered the telephone.

"Hello?"

"Ronni? It's Cole."

"Hi, Cole. Mom hasn't returned from her city council meeting tonight. Do you want me to have her return your call?"

"No, that's all right. I don't remember her telling me she had a meeting, though. I just wanted to let her know I'd be in tomorrow and to check in and see how things are going there."

"Everything seems to be going well. They've started tearing down walls in the other bedrooms in preparation for enlarging the bathrooms, I guess."

"Good, that's good. Lots of mess, I imagine?"

"Not too bad," Ronni said. "At least not yet."

"How's Aunt Claudia feeling about it all, now that the work is underway?"

"She seems more excited about it each day."

"I'm glad."

"Yes, so am I. She'll be happy you are coming back."

But how did Ronni feel about his return, Cole wondered. Did it even matter to her? "I'll be glad to get back there, too." When she didn't say anything, he asked, "How is your week going?"

"It's going well. I had a case of spring fever today and planted some flowers. I do love spring."

And I love you. The thought came to Cole sharp and clear, and his heart swelled with the knowledge that it was true. She wasn't ready to know how he felt. That much he was sure of.

"It's my favorite time of year, too. Everything seems to be budding out and blooming. What kind of flowers did you plant?"

"Oh, some Wave petunias along the walk, some salvia, and I even started a herb garden for Mom."

"Oh, she'll love that. I look forward to seeing everything bloom."

There was silence on the other end of the phone as if Ronni didn't know what to say next. Cole had plenty to say, but when he finally did let her know how he felt, he wanted to do it in person and not over the telephone lines.

He wanted to be able to take her in his arms and kiss her. "Guess I'd better let you go. Just tell Aunt Claudia I'll be in tomorrow afternoon and not to worry about making dinner. I'd like to take you both out."

"Okay, but—"

"Oh. . .and Ronni?" Cole interrupted her, afraid she was going to say she couldn't go.

"Yes?"

"Brian didn't deserve you. Not for one minute. I'll see you tomorrow." He didn't wait for a response. Instead, he gently ended the connection. Let her think about that.

※

Ronni looked at the receiver in her hand, her heart pounding against her ribs. Tears welled up in her eyes. Cole had just made her day, her week, and her month. He didn't think Brian's infidelity was her fault. She swallowed around the lump in her throat. Meagan had assured her of the same thing, just as Claudia had, but Cole's reassurance meant more to her than he would probably ever realize.

Deep down, Ronni knew that they all were right. Brian's weaknesses weren't her fault. He was just a very weak man. . .and probably more miserable with himself than anyone knew. She shook her head and released a deep sigh as she tried to let go of the past. Brian had paid a price for his weaknesses, and he was no longer here to hurt her. Maybe it was time for her to forgive him and get on with her life.

But that didn't mean she was ready to give her heart to another—even if it was trying to persuade her to do just that. Cole's opinion of her meant way more than she wanted it to. She had missed him and was glad he was coming back, but she didn't want him to know that. She didn't even want to admit it to herself, but there was no denying it.

She felt torn most of the time. Part of her wanted him here, and the other part of her knew she needed him to be as far away as possible.

"Ronni, is something wrong, dear?"

She hadn't heard Claudia drive up. She quickly hung up the phone. "Uh, no. Cole called. He'll be here tomorrow."

"Oh, wonderful! I'm sure that things are going well with the renovations, but I'll feel better if he checks them out."

"He said not to worry about making dinner. He wants to take us out. I didn't have a chance to tell him that tomorrow is my late night at the shop."

"Well, we can wait for you."

"No. There's no need for that. You two go on and enjoy yourselves."

"We'll see."

"How was your meeting, Mom?"

"It went really well. We've had some good applications for city manager, and after interviewing several, we've decided to offer the position to Dani Phillips."

"I don't recognize that name. Is that a woman or a man?"

Claudia chuckled. "D-A-N-I. She's a young woman about your age. She was born and raised here, and we were impressed with her desire to help Magnolia Bay. Not to mention that her salary requirements fit what we could pay."

"That's always a plus."

"Yes, it is." Claudia grinned.

They chatted for a while longer before calling it a night

and going upstairs. After checking out the work that had been done that day, they went to their rooms. Ronni was glad that Cole had planned for the renovations to the family quarters to be finished before updating the bathrooms in her and Claudia's current rooms.

She'd showered before Cole's telephone call, and on entering her room, she headed for the balcony. It looked out over the walking trail, and she couldn't help thinking of the last time she'd been on that trail with Cole. She'd been trying with all her might not to think of how wonderful it felt to be held in his arms. She'd never felt more protected and safe in her life, and she wanted to feel that way again.

But she had to stop thinking about it, about Cole. He was here because of Claudia—not because of her. Yet when he'd said what he did about Brian tonight. . .well, her heart just melted. *And—no!* She couldn't let herself care about Cole. She just couldn't. She looked heavenward.

"Dear Lord, please help me guard my heart. I'm in danger of losing it once more, and we know that my instincts were way off with Brian. Please, please help me to quench my growing attraction to his cousin. Please. In Jesus' name, amen."

twelve

Cole couldn't wait to get to his aunt's the next day. It was a good thing the car he'd rented at the airport had cruise control; otherwise, he'd have been sure to get a ticket for speeding. He'd dreamed about Ronni most of the night, and he still couldn't get her off his mind.

Just hearing her voice on the phone had him remembering how right it felt to hold her in his arms that night when he'd frightened her on the trail. Something about her brought out a surge of his protective instinct. He'd told her the truth last night: Brian hadn't deserved her. Plain and simple.

When he arrived at Melrose Manor, he was disappointed to find that Ronni wouldn't be going to eat with them that night, but he was relieved that it was because she had to work and not because she had just not wanted to. Having dinner with his aunt would give them a chance to discuss the day-to-day running of the inn, and they did need to do that. He'd just look forward to seeing Ronni later that evening.

The Seaside Surf and Turf was quickly becoming one of his favorite restaurants. There were many other nice restaurants between Magnolia Bay and Gulfport, but he was feeling very loyal to the town and didn't want to take his business elsewhere.

As they waited for their table, they ran into several city

council members who his aunt introduced him to, and he listened to them discuss the newest development—the hiring of a city manager. Apparently, they were on the verge of hiring a young woman for the position. He and Aunt Claudia were seated at a table and given menus before he could comment on the conversations.

"A lady city manager?" he asked.

"Yes, you don't have anything against hiring a woman—"

"Oh no, Aunt Claudia. I think whoever is best qualified for a job should get it. I just know there are some older men on the council, and I'm a bit surprised that *they* agreed to that."

"They did. Of course, the fact that most of them were friends of her late father probably didn't hurt her chances, but that aside, I think she's going to be a great city manager."

"If you think she will be, I'm sure you are right."

The waiter arrived to take their order, but as soon as he left, Aunt Claudia continued the conversation. "Dani Phillips will be a fine one; I am certain of it. And since you have no problem with hiring the best-qualified person for a position, I have an idea I'd like to run past you, Cole."

"Oh? What is it? You aren't going to ask for any major changes in the renovations, are you?"

Claudia chuckled. "No, dear, you gave me everything I wanted and more. I wouldn't do that to you at this late date, anyway. I wanted to talk to you about hiring a manager for the inn. If we can afford it, that is. I will be there, of course, but I'd like my role to be more as a hostess. And as we know from how long it took me to realize the trouble Brian had left me in, I don't have much of a head for record keeping."

She had a point, and Cole had figured they would need a manager. He just hadn't been sure of how to broach the subject, thinking his aunt might feel they wouldn't have enough money to pay one. He didn't see how they could afford *not* to hire someone. "We'll manage to pay for it. We can start advertising for a manager anytime now. In fact we should. It could take awhile to find the right person."

"No." Claudia shook her head. "No, that's not what I want to do. I want us to hire Ronni to manage the inn."

"Ronni?"

"Yes. She majored in business before she and Brian got married, but she's never really had a chance to put her training to use. When he died and she moved in with me, she just wanted a job to fill the hours and help us out. . .and be here for me, I believe. She's been Meagan's assistant manager at the shop—and that's been good for her—but I think we could really use her talents here."

"I didn't know she'd been a business major."

"Well, Brian didn't want her working. For some reason, he wanted it to appear that his wife didn't need to. And she didn't, or shouldn't have—except for his gambling. But it didn't seem to matter that she might want to. I believe she did, but she gave in to his wishes and tried to put her energies into being a good wife to him." Claudia paused and chewed her bottom lip.

Cole reached out and patted her hand. "It's all right, Aunt Claudia."

She sighed and shook her head before changing the subject. "Anyway, Ronni will inherit the inn when I'm gone, so she might as well have a hand in the running of it, don't you think?"

"Actually, I think that is a wonderful idea." Cole didn't add that the part he liked best was that he'd be able to see more of Ronni when he was in town, if she was there on the premises while all the work was being done. He had no doubts that she would be able to manage the inn. "Do you think she'll accept the position?"

"I don't know. She's very loyal, and she may not want to leave Meagan's shop. But I'm certainly going to be praying that she will."

"I'm all for it. When are you going to ask her?"

"We'll talk it over with her when she gets home tonight. Don't let me forget to order her some shrimp Alfredo before we leave. It's her favorite, and I promised her we'd bring her home something to eat."

"We'll put in the order when the waiter brings our dinners." He was glad to take something home for Ronni. He was anxious to see her again.

❧

Ronni parked her car behind Cole's and tried to convince her heart to quit beating double time just knowing he was back in Magnolia Bay. When she entered the kitchen and found Cole and Claudia seated at the table, Ronni prayed that she didn't give away how pleased she was at seeing him.

"Oh, good," Claudia said. "You are home. Let me get your dinner out of the warmer for you."

"I can do it, Mom. You stay put," Ronni said, putting her purse down and going over to the stove.

"Hi, Ronni," Cole said. "It's good to see you. I wish you could have gone with us tonight."

"Thank you, Cole." *It's wonderful to see you, too.* Ronni bent to retrieve her food from the warming drawer.

"Mmm, this smells delicious. Thank you for bringing it home for me."

She joined them at the table and noticed the plans lying out before them. "What are you two up to? You aren't changing anything, are you?"

"No. Just checking to make sure things are moving ahead the way they are supposed to. I checked everything they are doing, and it's all looking good."

Ronni began to eat while Cole and Claudia talked about the renovations.

"The new bathrooms are taking shape. You'll have to check them out when you go upstairs, Ronni." Claudia chuckled. "Our nightly ritual now is to check out what has been done during the day. It's fascinating to see the progress."

"I'm glad we chose Jim's company," Cole said. "He's doing a really good job."

"He sure seems to know what he's doing from what I can tell." Ronni didn't want them to think she wasn't interested in what was going on. "Of course I'm not here as much as Mom is, so she would know better than I do, but it's going much smoother than I anticipated."

"Jim is a good man, and he's got a good crew working for him." Claudia added, "But as for you not being here. . .well, we have a proposal we'd like to talk over with you, dear."

"Oh? What kind of proposal?" Ronni's shrimp Alfredo–filled fork stopped midway to her mouth.

"It can wait until you've eaten."

"Uh-oh. That doesn't sound good."

"Oh, but we think it is. For us, anyway," Cole said, smiling at her.

"What is it? I can eat while you tell me about it." Ronni took the bite of her shrimp Alfredo to prove her point.

"Well, you know I don't have much of a head for business," Claudia said. "I think the last few months prove that. I should have come to you when I first suspected trouble, Ronni, but because it involved Brian—"

"There isn't more trouble, is there?" Ronni asked.

"No, dear. Everything is going well. It doesn't have anything to do with that. We—"

"What Aunt Claudia is trying to say is that we'd like you to think about becoming the inn's manager."

"The manager?"

"Yes. You are the perfect person for the job, Ronni."

"But, I—I don't know what to say." She would love the job of managing the inn. She had so many ideas, but she hadn't voiced most of them because she didn't feel it was her place to do so.

"I know it would be hard for you to quit working for Meagan. But we really do need a manager, and you are the only person I trust enough to offer the position."

"Oh, Mom—"

"Just think about it, please."

"We'd pay you more than you are making now," Cole offered with a grin. "Since all of this is part yours anyway, I'm sure Meagan will understand."

She probably would. But Meagan had given her a job when she badly needed one, and Ronni didn't want to put her in a bind. Besides all of that, there was the fact that if she were working around here, she would see much more of Cole. She wasn't sure her heart was ready for more contact with him. She was having enough problems with it as it was.

"Just think about it, Ronni dear, won't you?"

"Yes, please do. We don't have to have an answer tonight. Just don't turn us down until you really consider it." Cole's gaze met hers.

Ronni almost bit her tongue to keep from agreeing on the spot. She really didn't know what to do, and she couldn't say yes until she did. She needed some time to herself to mull it all over. "Thank you. I promise I will think on it and pray about it."

"That's all we can ask of you, dear. I'm sure you'll make the right decision," Claudia said, getting up from the table. "We won't hound you about it. How about some key lime pie for dessert? Cole insisted we buy enough for the three of us to share."

Ronni was glad to change the subject for the moment. "Mmm, my favorite! I'd love a piece! But I'll have to save some of this for another time if I'm going to have room for pie."

Ronni shut the container her meal had come in and put it in the refrigerator while Cole got up to help his aunt get the dessert. All kinds of emotions whirled around inside Ronni. She wanted to accept their offer. It would be wonderful to be here and see the inn take shape and to be a part of the whole experience. But as Cole set her dessert plate in front of her with a flourish, as if he were a waiter, his arm brushed hers, and she wasn't sure she could be in close proximity to this man and keep her heart whole. She was afraid he may have already laid claim to part of it.

ॐ

Ronni became quieter as the evening wore on, and Cole wondered if he was the cause of her hesitancy over taking the offer. Then he told himself he was probably placing too much importance on his presence in her life. Maybe he just wanted to think he mattered more to her than he actually did. More than likely, she was just concerned about letting Meagan down.

Still, when Ronni called it a night and headed upstairs, he broached the subject with his aunt. "Do you think Ronni's hesitancy has anything to do with me, Aunt Claudia?"

"No. I don't think so. Why would it?"

"Well, she just seems. . .she's not totally comfortable around me."

His aunt sighed and leaned toward him. "Cole, it's not you—or at least not only you. I don't think Ronni is at ease around most men these days. Because of my son, she doesn't find it easy to trust men as a group. It hurts me to tell you that he treated her badly. But he did. You know that, anyway. Ronni and I don't talk about it much. Never have. I think we both want to spare the other more heartache. Most of the time I try not to think about it. I don't want to confront the fact that my son was not a good man."

Cole's heart broke all over again for Ronni and for his aunt. "I'm sorry, Aunt Claudia. I didn't mean to cause you any pain."

"Cole, it's not your fault. It's my son's. And I have to carry part of the blame myself. I must have failed somewhere along the way."

"Aunt Claudia, none of this has been your fault. We all have choices in life. Brian made wrong ones. You didn't make them for him."

His aunt dabbed at tears that had escaped from the corners of her eyes. "I just hope that Ronni will take this position. I've already had her named as my beneficiary when I pass away. And I've named you as the executor of my will. I hope that's all right."

"You know it is, Aunt Claudia."

"I want her future assured, Cole."

"I can promise you that I will do all I can to see that it is." And he wouldn't mind one bit if Ronni's future included him—if he could ever gain her trust.

"Thank you. I think I'll call it a night, too."

Cole stood when she did and gave her a kiss on the cheek. "Night, Aunt Claudia. I hope you sleep well."

"I will if I leave it all in the Lord's hands. Sometimes it's been hard for me to give up control of things, but I have learned that when I truly leave everything in His hands, they turn out much better than they do in mine. Good night."

Cole watched as she headed upstairs and thought how much he still had to learn from her. He'd never known anyone to age as gracefully as his aunt had, and she seemed to get wiser with each passing year.

He went to the utility room off the kitchen where he'd taken to leaving his jogging shoes and put them on. There was no way he was going to be able to sleep for a while. Too many things were whirling around in his mind. He went outside and did some stretches before beginning his jog.

He hoped Ronni took them up on the offer to manage the inn. He'd love to spend more time with her. Maybe if she got to know him better, she'd begin to trust him. He wondered if it would be easier to gain her trust if he weren't related to Brian, but he had a feeling his aunt was right and it was just going to be hard for Ronni to have confidence in any man again.

That didn't mean it would never happen. It might just take persistence in convincing her that he was trustworthy—and faith that she eventually would look at him that way. But knowing he couldn't do it alone, Cole prayed: *Dear Lord, please heal the hurts Brian inflicted on both Aunt Claudia and especially on Ronni. I pray that she will be able to trust her heart again—to me, of course, as I know I am falling in love with her. But You already know that. If it is Your will, I pray she might begin to see me as someone who would never treat her like Brian did. . .someone who would honor her always. And, Lord, please help me to do as Aunt Claudia has learned to do: give control to You. In Jesus' name, amen.*

thirteen

Ronni managed to get downstairs before either Cole or Claudia the next morning. Normally, she didn't have to go in early on the day after she worked late, but she needed time to think, to make a decision about the position she'd been offered. She wanted time alone to try and figure out what to do. She'd tossed and turned most of the night until she'd finally prayed for the Lord to guide her in making the right decision.

She stopped at the coffee shop for breakfast, and after giving her order for a ham omelet and coffee, she pulled a notebook out of her purse and started making a list of pros and cons to becoming the inn's manager.

Under the pro list, she wrote:

1. *Being able to actually use the degree I worked hard for and have never been able to use.*
2. *Being able to see the renovations take place and share the excitement of a new venture.*
3. *Being able to feel I have a right to voice my opinions about the running of the inn—even though Claudia welcomes my input.*

Ronnie shook her head. She knew that one didn't make any sense.

Being able to see Cole more often. No. She couldn't write

that down. Still, the thought was there, and it didn't go away.

Under the con list, she wrote:

1. Letting down Meagan.

Seeing too much of Cole. No. She couldn't write that down, either. But the thought was there.

Evidently Cole canceled himself out and didn't need to be part of her decision. Ronni sighed. She did want to manage the inn. She'd been excited about the prospect ever since Cole and Claudia had offered the position to her the night before. It would be challenging and exciting, and as much as she loved Meagan and didn't want to disappoint her, she really wanted and needed a change. She looked over her list. The pros did outweigh the cons, with or without Cole added to the mix.

The waitress brought her breakfast to the table, and once she'd left, Ronni offered a silent prayer for the Lord to let her know if she'd made the wrong decision and to help her explain it all to Meagan if she'd made the right one.

By the time she got to work, she'd practiced what she would say several times.

"Hey, Ronni!" Meagan called. "What are you doing here at this time? You aren't due in for another hour."

"I have something I'd like to run by you if you have a minute."

Meagan called Laura out of the stockroom. "Can you watch up front for a minute while Ronni and I take a break?"

"Sure I can. Morning, Ronni," Laura said.

"Good morning, Laura."

"If my ten o'clock comes in early, just come and get me," Meagan said as they headed for the kitchen. She sat down at the table and motioned for Ronni to do the same. "Sit down and tell me what's on your mind."

Ronni took a chair and then took a deep breath.

"What's wrong, Ronni?" Meagan's brow furrowed with concern.

"Nothing is wrong. I just don't know how to tell you—"

"Tell me what? You aren't quitting, are you?"

"Well. . .oh, Meagan, you have always been there for me, and you gave me a job when I needed one so badly. But Claudia and Cole have offered me the manager's position at the inn."

There. It was out. She held her breath, waiting for Meagan's response.

"Oh, Ronni! I hate to lose you, but I know that is something you would be wonderful at! And you do have a personal interest in the inn. I certainly understand why you would want to take them up on their offer."

Ronni let out the breath she'd been holding in a loud *whoosh*. "You do?"

Meagan chuckled. "Of course I do. You didn't think I was going to take it that bad, did you?"

"I just didn't want to disappoint you."

"Well, I will miss you. But there is no way I'd tell you not to take that position."

"Oh, thank you, Meagan. I just didn't want to make things hard for you. And I can work until you find a replacement if you need me to."

"I think we'll be okay. Now that I've moved my home

office here, it's made life much easier. I think I can get by without an assistant manager since I'm working here on the premises. And if I see that I do need one, I'll promote Laura or Sara and hire someone to take their place. If you can work the rest of this week and give me a chance to maybe bring in a part-time employee, I think that will work. Actually, Tori has been hinting for a part-time job." Meagan grinned. "Now just might be her chance."

"Oh, Meagan, I am going to miss working with you! But I thank you so much for understanding."

"I really am happy for you, Ronni. This is a great opportunity. And who knows? We might get to do more together if you aren't working here."

"That would be wonderful!" They'd become close enough that Ronni knew Meagan meant what she said. And it would be nice to be able to get together outside of work more often.

Ronni could barely contain her excitement for the rest of the day. She almost picked up the telephone to tell Claudia what she'd decided but then told herself that it would be more fun in person.

Meagan must have sensed her anticipation because she insisted Ronni take off an hour early. "You started work before you were supposed to. It's only right you go home now. Besides, you don't have any color consultations scheduled for this afternoon—so go. Just remember to call me later and let me know what they say, okay?"

Ordinarily, Ronni wouldn't have thought about going home early, but today was an exception. She couldn't concentrate on work, anyway. "I will!"

If she remembered right, this was the afternoon the city

council was going to offer the city manager job to Dani Phillips, so she was pretty sure that Claudia hadn't started anything for dinner yet. She'd like to surprise her and Cole by making the meal.

Ronni stopped by the store and picked up the makings for lasagna. She seemed to be in the mood for Italian, lately. When she pulled up at home, it was to find that both Claudia's and Cole's cars were gone. The workers were hard at it, though, if the sound reverberating throughout the house was any indication. From the sound of it, they were having a grand time either tearing something down or putting it up.

She'd take a look later, but first she wanted to get her meat sauce going. She chopped onions while the ground beef and Italian sausage browned, then added the onions along with some minced garlic and other spices. After adding the tomatoes and tomato sauce, she worked in a can of tomato paste and brought it all to a boil before lowering the heat, putting a lid on the pan, and letting the sauce simmer.

Ronni then made a salad and put it in the refrigerator, and she was putting water on to boil for the lasagna noodles when Cole came inside.

"Ronni, I didn't expect to find you home." He sniffed appreciatively. "Mmm, that smells delicious. Are you the cook tonight?"

"I thought I'd give Mom a break. And I just had an urge to cook."

"I'm sure Aunt Claudia will be thrilled," he said, approaching the stove. "Are we having spaghetti?"

"No," Ronni said, lifting the lid to the sauce and stirring, just to give herself something to do. She was afraid if she just stood there, he might be able to hear the pounding of her heart. "We're having lasagna."

"Mmm, one of my favorites. She said she'd be back by six. I hope she's not late."

Ronni couldn't help but chuckle. Claudia had been right. It was fun to cook for a hungry man.

"Sounds like the workers are about to quit for the day. Want to check things out?"

Ronni looked at the bubbling water. "Let me get the lasagna in the oven, and then I can. I'll meet you up there if you want to go ahead."

"I would like to catch Jim before he leaves for the day. Come on up when you can."

"I will." She slipped the noodles into the boiling water and grated the mozzarella cheese while she waited for the pasta to cook. Finally, she put some meat sauce into the bottom of a lasagna pan and began layering the noodles, meat sauce, and different cheeses. She popped the pan into the oven just as Claudia walked in the door.

"Ronni! You are home early and. . ." She inhaled deeply. "You are making your wonderful lasagna for dinner. Mmm."

"I thought it was time I gave you a break."

"Well, thank you, dear. I do appreciate it." She dropped her purse on the counter and slipped out of her high heels. "Where is Cole?"

"He's upstairs checking the day's progress. I was supposed to go up when I got dinner in the oven."

"Well, let's join him now," Claudia said. "I think they are putting in the tile in the new bathrooms."

She was right. The floors had been installed. Ronni

loved the neutral tones of the twelve-inch ceramic tiles. The stand-alone basins and new showers had been put in earlier in the week, and once the grout in the floors had a chance to dry and be sealed, the new bathrooms on this floor would be finished.

"Tomorrow, we'll be putting the new tubs in your bathrooms, so you might want to clear out some of your personal things this evening," Jim said before he took off for the night.

"I can't believe they are nearly through with this floor," Claudia said.

"The family quarters are going to take longer," Cole reminded her. "And then there are the kitchen updates downstairs. This is really just the beginning, but how do you like everything so far?"

"I love it all," Ronni said as they all started back downstairs. "These rooms are going to make lovely guest accommodations."

"I'd like you to help me decide what furniture to use in them and what needs to be recovered when you have time, Ronni, if you would," Claudia said.

"Of course I'll help," Ronni answered. She didn't want to tell them her decision just yet, so she hurried into the kitchen. "From the smell of things, dinner will be ready as soon as I get the garlic bread made and the salad out."

"I'll help. I know how to spread butter," Cole said.

Actually Cole took over making the garlic bread while Ronni set the table, filled the tea glasses, and took the lasagna out of the oven. Claudia pulled the salad out of the refrigerator and put it on the table. By the time the bread was toasty, they were more than ready to eat.

Cole said a prayer, and they each served themselves from the large pan Ronni had placed on a trivet. There wasn't much conversation for the first few minutes.

"This is delicious, Ronni," Cole said after his first several bites. "That smell made its way up to the second floor, and I thought for a minute that Jim was going to invite himself to dinner."

"Thank you," Ronni said. "I'm not the chef Mom is, but I do enjoy cooking."

"You cook every bit as well as I do. I just don't give you a chance to very often, do I?" Claudia didn't seem to expect an answer as she continued. "This is wonderful."

"How did your meeting go? Did you offer the position to Dani?" Ronni asked.

"We did. She was so excited about it." Claudia smiled. "I think she's going to make a wonderful city manager."

"Speaking of positions," Cole said, his gaze capturing Ronni's, "have you made a decision about becoming the inn manager yet?"

"Cole, we said we wouldn't pressure her," Claudia said.

"It's all right, Mom." They'd both tried to give her time; she knew that. But she needed to give them her answer. "Actually, I have made up my mind."

The clink of cutlery stopped. "And what did you decide, dear?" Claudia prompted.

"I told Meagan today that I would like to accept your offer. She was wonderful about it."

Claudia chuckled and clapped her hands. "I am so glad!"

"I figured Meagan would be supportive of you. She's a nice lady," Cole added.

Ronni had almost forgotten that he and Meagan had

known each other a long time. Cole knew Meagan better than she did. But she agreed wholeheartedly with his assessment of Meagan's character. "She certainly is. She told me to give her a week, so. . .I can probably get started here next week."

"That is absolutely great news," Cole said. "Especially, as I have to go back to Dallas this next week. I'll be checking on things as best I can."

Ronni's heart dropped, and her elated mood seemed to collapse at his news. Yet she knew she should be relieved instead of disappointed that he would be going back to Texas. It was just that the house had begun to feel empty when he wasn't around. And this afternoon, she'd really liked that he was upstairs while she was making dinner downstairs. It was a comforting feeling somehow. She simply liked knowing he was there.

"I do wish you didn't have to go back so soon." Claudia voiced Ronni's feelings perfectly.

"So do I. But I won't stay there any longer than I have to, and I'll check in with you each night. I'll be anxious to know what's going on here. What are you going to do first, Ronni?"

"I think I need to line up suppliers for the food and linens," Ronni answered. "Contact travel agencies and get our name out there. What is going to be our name? Are we sticking with Melrose Manor?"

"Oh, I don't think so. But that's something we need to decide, isn't it? See, you've already got a handle on things I hadn't even thought of," Claudia said.

"Do either of you have an idea for the name?" Cole asked. At the simultaneous shake of their heads, he threw out a few suggestions. "How about Magnolia Manor? Or Melrose Inn?"

"What about Magnolia Bay Inn?" Claudia asked.

"That's good. I was thinking just Bay Inn, but I like yours better," Ronni insisted.

"Well, it's a mouthful. Bay Inn is short and sweet. I like it," Claudia said.

"Magnolia Manor, Melrose Inn, Magnolia Bay Inn, Bay Inn. . ." Cole repeated them all. "I like Bay Inn, too. It's easy to say, and it will be easy to remember."

"Let's go with it, then," Claudia said.

"You're sure?" Ronni asked.

She and Cole looked at Claudia as she nodded. "Yes. Bay Inn, it is."

Ronni grinned, feeling exceptionally pleased that they liked her suggestion. She was feeling like Bay Inn's manager already.

❧

Cole had about given up on Ronni ever joining him for a jog. He waited for about ten minutes like he always did, but she didn't show up. Not that he expected her to, but still, he hoped.

As he started jogging down the path, he dreaded leaving again. But what he hadn't told his aunt or Ronni was that he'd been out looking for office space that afternoon. He thought he'd found the perfect spot, but he needed to work up some plans on the changes he'd want to make if he took it.

He'd almost made up his mind to relocate here in Magnolia Bay. He could work from anywhere, but he'd like his home base to be closer to his aunt, as she was all the family he had left—not to mention he liked that Ronni was here, too. He had loved coming home to find her in the kitchen today. He certainly hadn't realized what an excellent chef she was. She'd said she liked to cook, and he had a feeling that she would like to cook more but that because his aunt enjoyed cooking, too, Ronni gave most of it over to her. Another instance of how much she cared about Aunt Claudia.

He was more than happy that Ronni had accepted the position as manager. She'd even come up with the perfect name and seemed really pleased when they'd agreed on it. She looked truly happy tonight. He wished she could look that way all the time.

Much as he hated having to leave, he did feel better knowing that Ronni would be helping Claudia oversee the work. He couldn't make the move here overnight and would have to continue going back and forth for a while yet. But the idea of calling Magnolia Bay home appealed to him more and more each day.

fourteen

During the next few weeks as Cole flew between Texas, to oversee his business, and Mississippi, to check on the progress on Bay Inn, he became increasingly convinced he should move back to Magnolia Bay. He would still have to travel some, but not as much if he had his headquarters in Mississippi. Some of his clients flew into Texas; they could just as well fly into Mississippi.

It was becoming more difficult to leave his aunt. . .and especially Ronni. The nightly phone calls were just not the same as being there. He felt like he was missing out on too much by being in Texas.

Ronni seemed to be in her element as manager of Bay Inn. She'd already put suppliers in place, looked into some local advertising, and contacted travel agents all over the country. And she was in the process of designing a Web site for the inn.

When Aunt Claudia had first brought up hiring Ronni, Cole had been all for it just because she would be part owner of the inn, anyway. But mostly he'd liked the idea because he thought he'd be seeing more of Ronni. What he didn't realize was what his aunt obviously knew: Ronni was an excellent businesswoman.

Cole's days in Dallas seemed to drag, but the time in Magnolia Bay sped by like a lightning flash. It seemed he no more than got there until it was time to leave again. He needed to be here more than he was in Texas if he was ever going to get Ronni to see that he was in love with her.

On this late April day, as he drove down the familiar Bay Drive on his way to the inn, he had no doubt that he was in love with Ronni—deeply and completely. He would love nothing more than to be able to share his life with her. He sighed deeply. Her disillusionment with marriage came long before Brian's death, and just finding out that he'd been unfaithful to her during that time made it even worse. He couldn't blame her for being afraid to trust her heart to anyone again.

But oh, how he wanted to be that man if she ever did decide to trust and fall in love again. Cole had no idea how he was ever going to persuade her that he was nothing like Brian. All he could do was pray that the Lord would help him convince her that he would treasure her all the days of their lives—and try to see as much of her as possible, hoping that she would begin to care about him, too.

He turned down the drive that led to his aunt's home, noticing that everything had gone from bud to bloom since the last time he had been there. The azaleas colored the grounds along with the daylilies. He wondered how Ronni's flowers were doing. Aunt Claudia had told him that Ronni was turning into quite a gardener.

His heart seemed to expand when he rounded the drive to the back of the inn and found Ronni's car there. He couldn't wait to see her.

He could hear the workmen upstairs, but the first place he looked for Ronni was in the study. They'd set up a new computer for her in there. Aunt Claudia had moved her things upstairs to the desk in her room for the time being.

Ronni was staring at the computer screen intently and wasn't aware he'd come into the room. Not wanting to frighten her, he knocked on the door frame and cleared his throat. When she turned and saw him there, the smile she gave him had his heart doing a somersault. For a brief moment, he felt as if she was as glad to see him as he was to see her. He wanted to rush over and take her in his arms—but she blinked, and the moment was gone. It was as if a curtain had fallen over her face, and he could no longer tell what she was feeling. He'd probably imagined it, anyway.

"Hi, Ronni. It's good to see you. What are you working on?"

"Hi, Cole. I've been working on our Web site. It needs more work, but come see what you think of it."

Cole crossed the room and looked over her shoulder. She smelled wonderful—like the fresh flowers and herbs from her gardens, but he didn't tell her that. Instead he looked at the different pages she brought up on the computer screen. She'd done a magnificent job. The pictures she'd taken with her digital camera showed how beautiful Bay Inn's grounds were. She'd snapped them from the front, the back, each side, and from the balconies. It was like seeing it all with new eyes.

"Once the rooms are finished, I'll put pictures of them up, too." Ronni turned her head to see his response.

His reaction to her was to want to tip her face up and kiss her, but he cleared his throat instead. "I think you've captured the beauty and tranquility of the estate. I'm seeing things in a whole new way, and I want to make a reservation today."

Ronni chuckled and turned back to the computer. "I think that can be arranged."

She did seem to be a little more comfortable around him these days, and for that he was extremely grateful. But now, she seemed to see him as a business partner. Aunt Claudia's nephew, Brian's cousin, Meagan's longtime friend, and now as a business professional—Cole wondered if she would ever see him as a man who had lost his heart to her.

Probably not unless I give her a hint that it's happening. He didn't know where the thought came from, but it opened his eyes. He had gone out of his way to keep from scaring her away, but he just now realized that he might have done too good a job of it. What if she had no idea how he felt? Furthermore, what if some other eligible man came to stay at the inn and, without knowing her past hurts, put his all into convincing her to give him a chance? No! He couldn't let that happen.

"Cole?" Ronni's voice brought him back from his runaway thoughts.

"Yes?"

"Is something wrong? You look kind of funny."

Like in a panic, probably. And that's exactly how he felt—panicked. But he tried to hide it. "I'm all right. Just thinking."

"Oh, okay." She smiled at him. "I'm glad you like what I'm doing with the Web site."

"I do." Was it time to give her a hint about how he felt? Cole reached out and tucked an errant curl behind her ear. Her eyes widened, but she didn't jerk away. "Have I told you that I'm very glad you are going to manage the inn? I like every idea you've come up with."

"I. . .uh, thank you—"

"Ronni, Cole, I'm home," Aunt Claudia called from the kitchen. "My meeting ran longer than I thought it would."

Cole turned at the sound of his aunt's footsteps nearing the study, and he crossed the room to meet her at the door. Bending to kiss her on the cheek, he was glad to see her looking so good. "I figured you were out and about. How is the new city manager working out?"

"She's doing a great job. . .just as Ronni is in her new position. Did you see what she's doing on the Internet?"

"I did. We made an excellent decision in asking her to become Bay Inn's manager." Cole smiled, and as his gaze met Ronni's, he could see a hint of color flood her cheeks. Maybe she wasn't as immune to him as he thought. He certainly hoped not. Could be his small hint might have her thinking about him a little differently. If not, he might have to come up with a bigger one, because he didn't think he could hide his growing love from her much longer.

☙

Ronni tried to will her heart to slow down. Ever since Cole had come into the room, she'd been having trouble breathing normally. His presence seemed to practically take her breath away.

Feeling herself blush at the look he gave her, she turned back to the computer and tried to appear busy while they talked about Claudia's city council meeting. All Ronni could think about was the brush of Cole's fingertips against her cheek when he tucked her hair behind her ear. That small touch had sent a bolt of electricity right down her spine.

Maybe she had made a mistake in taking this job. She'd

been trying hard to ignore the way her pulse raced when she answered the phone and heard his voice on the other end of the line and the way her heart jumped when she came in to find him at the kitchen table—or when he surprised them by coming back earlier than expected, as he had today.

She didn't know how she was going to be able to hide her reactions to him much longer—especially if he continued to look at her the way he had just now. There was something different in his expression today, and she wasn't sure what it was. But it had her heart beating double time just thinking about it.

"Let's go to the Seaside Surf and Turf for dinner," Cole said. "Is that all right with you, Ronni?"

Afraid he'd read her interest in her eyes, Ronni pretended to be very involved in her computer program. "That's fine with me. What time do I need to be ready?"

"She puts in so many hours on that computer," Claudia said, unaware that she was helping Ronni's pretense look real. "I just couldn't do it. My eyes would give out on me."

"She needs to take a break, then," Cole said from behind her. He tugged at the hair she had pulled back from her face. "Can you be ready by six thirty?"

Ronni was having trouble breathing. So intent had she been on making it look like she was hard at work that she hadn't heard him cross the room to stand right behind her. "I can."

"Good. We'll leave you at it, but if you aren't out of here in about thirty minutes, I'll be back to get you."

It was only after Cole and Claudia had left the room that Ronni began to breathe normally again. She was more than a little attracted to Cole Bannister, and she didn't know what to do about it. She had promised herself that she would not let herself care for anyone ever again. She didn't want to fall in love, didn't want to open her heart up for being hurt again. And she had no business at all in being so attracted to Cole. His life was in Dallas, and after Bay Inn was open, he would be coming here much less often.

Even if Cole were attracted to her and even if he cared, she couldn't just go off and leave Claudia. Ronni had to chuckle at herself. There sure were a lot of *if*s in her thoughts.

Then she turned somber. She knew already that *if*s got one nowhere. *If* Brian hadn't loved to gamble and drink, he might still be here. *If* he hadn't left his mother in such a mess, they might not be turning her home into a place of business. . .nice as it was going to be. And *if* Ronni hadn't been so hurt by him, she might be willing to try love again. But the very thought of being that vulnerable again frightened her in every fiber of her being. Yet when she thought of Cole, she was very much afraid she was already more than halfway there.

fifteen

By the end of May, Cole couldn't believe the renovations on Bay Inn were nearly finished. Everything had gone more smoothly than he'd anticipated, and he was quite pleased at the quality of the craftsmanship. The work on the kitchen and the second story was finished, and only a few things remained to be finished in the family quarters. Jim and his people had put their all into getting Bay Inn ready for a June 15 grand opening. It looked like they were right on target.

Most of what was left to do was the decorating of the family quarters, and Ronni and his aunt were having the time of their lives doing just that. If he'd looked at one paint sample, he'd looked at a hundred, it seemed. And he'd never seen so many fabric swatches in his life. But his fun came in watching them decide.

They were still at it when he came back from his jog. . . something he hadn't been able to convince Ronni to join him in doing yet. Tonight, they were trying to pick fabrics for drapes and furnishings in the family quarters. The guest rooms had been top priority, and they were all finished and just waiting for guests. Cole didn't know how she'd done it—Aunt Claudia had told him it was by "the sweat of her brow and burning the midnight oil"—but Ronni had managed to book the inn solid from grand opening until at least Labor Day.

He got himself a bottle of water from the restaurant-sized refrigerator that had been installed a week ago and joined them in the study. Fabric swatches were all over the place as the two women sat on the sofa and held up one and then another solid-colored swatch next to a flowered print they both seemed to like.

"Cole! Good, you're here, and you can help decide which colors to go with for the family dining room," Aunt Claudia said.

He held up a hand as he took a seat in one of the leather chairs. "Oh no. I'm not getting in on this. I don't do fabrics."

"Cole, dear, you'll be staying in the family quarters when you are here, too. We'd like your input, wouldn't we, Ronni?"

Ronni looked up from the swatch she was studying. She seemed a little. . .lost in thought. "Of course."

"See?"

"No, Aunt Claudia." He tried to sound firm. "I will like anything the two of you agree on. I promise."

"Cole—"

"I'm going upstairs now, Aunt Claudia. That jog just wore me out." He started to back out of the room but stopped in his tracks at Ronni's giggle.

"I don't think Cole wants to be blamed if we regret any of our choices later, Mom. I can't say I blame him, either."

"You read me well, Ronni," he said. But he wondered how she could seem to understand him that well and not know that it was all he could do to keep from taking her in his arms and telling her he loved her. Maybe she needed another small hint. He looked her in the eye. "I just want you to be happy."

He was rewarded by seeing a delicate shade of pink flood her cheeks.

"One more thing, Cole." His aunt called his attention back to her. "We have an idea we need to run by you."

"Aunt Claudia, you don't need my input in the decorating," he insisted. He'd hired a decorator for his own home—he could design just about any kind of building, but he left the actual decorating to others. "Really."

"No, dear, it's not that. We've been thinking we'd like to have a pre-grand-opening party for some of our close friends. Just to let them all see what we've done and let this old house get used to being full of people again."

"I like that idea a lot."

"Oh good!" Claudia said. "Ronni and I thought you'd like it, but before we sent out any invitations, we wanted to make sure you'd be here."

"When were you planning it?"

"We weren't sure. The week before. . .or even the night before, if that would work better for you."

"When is the opening?"

"Two weeks from tomorrow," Ronni said with a yawn.

"Why don't we have it next weekend? That will give you time to rest up before the opening."

His aunt nodded. "Okay. Ronni said she thought that would be best, too."

"Good. I'm going to call it a night. Happy fabric choosing, ladies. Don't stay up too late." With that, he chuckled and walked out of the room.

ઢ

Ronni's heart was still racing when she went upstairs and got ready for bed. She was sure she was reading too much into Cole's words, but when he'd said he wanted her to be happy and had looked at her so intently, her heart had jump-started into overdrive and hadn't beat like normal since.

It was probably a good thing that Cole wasn't here all the time, although much as she'd like to deny it, she missed him terribly when he was in Texas. It was all she could do to sound normal when he called. She felt breathless most of the time. He even asked her once if she'd run to answer the phone.

She kept telling herself that she'd made a pact never to fall in love again, but she couldn't seem to keep from caring about Cole. She looked forward to his calls at night and to telling him about all the work being done on the inn—about how excited Claudia was getting, how good the cook they'd hired was, and any number of things that went on while he was gone. Then somehow, when he came back to Magnolia Bay, she had a hard time talking to him about much of anything.

She knew it was because she didn't have to worry about him being able to see her reaction to his voice over the telephone. He couldn't see the telltale blush that crept up her neck to her face, couldn't see the way she closed her eyes and just enjoyed hearing him talk, and he wasn't close enough to hear the pounding of her heart.

But when he was here in person, she felt she had to guard against giving away her growing feelings for him. And she was afraid it was only a matter of time until he found out.

Then what? The tenuous relationship they were forming would have to change, and she wasn't sure in what way.

Maybe he would stop coming if he found out how much she cared. Yet she felt that he was attracted to her, too. Just in the last few weeks, he'd been saying things and looking at her in ways that had her averting her face, changing the subject so that he couldn't see the heat rise in her cheeks or tell how flustered she would get around him at times.

She shook her head as she prepared for bed. She had to quit thinking about him, had to convince herself that she didn't care. Ronni loved her position as manager here, loved helping turn the manor into what would be a grand inn, and she didn't want to have to give it up. But when what she looked forward to most was Cole's visits, seeing him each day, sharing meals with him, going to church with him and Claudia, and just knowing he was there. . .she wasn't sure she'd be able to stay at the inn. Didn't know how much longer she could fight her growing attraction to him. Once she was found out, would she have to give up the job she loved?

She prayed not. And she prayed that the Lord would help quench her growing feelings for Cole. But deep down, what she really wanted was to let herself fall in love with him and for him to love her back.

ès

By the end of the week, Cole was ready to move to Magnolia Bay. Just the thought of leaving again was depressing to him. But the move couldn't be done overnight, and he didn't want to mention it to his aunt or Ronni until he was certain it was what he was going to do.

The week had passed much too fast. They'd gone to church on Sunday and then out to dinner with the Chamberses again. He liked Nick a lot. Much as he'd hated seeing his best friend in Dallas be jilted by Meagan, he could see that she and Nick were meant to be together.

He could only hope for a relationship that good one day. And he knew exactly who he wanted to have it with. *Ronni*. Each day he looked forward to seeing her and was very happy they'd talked her into managing the inn—if for no other reason than that she didn't run off to work in town each day. Oh, she might try to avoid him from time to time, but since she worked in the study right off the kitchen, it wasn't hard to find her at some point during the day.

She was a busy woman, getting ready for the party for their friends this weekend and the upcoming grand opening of Bay Inn on the next. He had watched Ronni and his aunt add all the finishing touches to the guest rooms and public areas downstairs once they'd moved their personal things up to the family quarters, which were done except for the decorating. They could work on those finishing touches for months to come. He liked the room they'd given him. It looked out over the bay and was quite comfortable and cozy.

On Thursday, he'd taken them out to dinner, trying to give them a much-needed break. His aunt and Ronni were preparing all of the party food, and they'd been doing a run-through of the finger foods. The new cook, Marge Acorn, would be there for the grand opening, and after that, Marge would prepare dinners at the inn. His aunt had decided to do the breakfasts, and she would try to send the guests into town for lunch, thereby helping local businesses, too. They were having the party on Friday instead of Saturday, because he'd insisted they needed the whole weekend to rest before gearing up for the grand opening.

Today, they'd kept him busy all day, running errands and manning the telephone while they laid out the buffet tables. Now as their guests began to arrive, he still didn't know how his aunt and Ronni had pulled everything together. But they had, and the house had never looked more inviting.

The first guests to arrive were Meagan, Nick, and his grandmother and sister. Then Claudia's friends from the city council began to show up. The new city manager was there as were the sheriff and chief of police. The owners of the Seaside Surf and Turf, Mike and Alice Benson, came, as did several of Ronni's former coworkers from Meagan's Color Cottage.

Before long, people were milling around everywhere except the family quarters and in the downstairs study, checking out the changes in what was now Bay Inn. Finger foods and desserts were set up in the dining room and both living areas, and Cole was pleased that the flow through the rooms lent itself to large gatherings.

"I was a little worried that it would feel crowded with this many people, but it feels quite comfortable, don't you think?" his aunt asked as he helped himself to several finger sandwiches.

"I think this home was meant for entertaining and lots of guests, Aunt Claudia. It's going to become known as one of the best B&Bs in the South."

"I think so, too—especially with Ronni managing it."

"You're right. I'm glad you insisted on offering the position to her."

"So am I," Ronni said from behind. "Thank you both for putting such confidence in me. I promise I'm going to do my very best to live up to your expectations."

"You already have, dear. I'm glad we decided to have this party. It puts my mind at rest that this old home of ours will be able to welcome people through its doors for years to come. I can't wait until next weekend and the grand opening."

"Neither can I," Ronni said.

"It will be here before you know it. I'm glad I can stay until after the opening at least." He didn't want to go back. Not even for a few days. It was going to be hard enough to leave after the opening.

"Are you all over here congratulating yourselves for this magnificent new inn?" Meagan asked as she and Nick walked up. "You deserve to, for sure."

"Bay Inn is going to be a wonderful bonus to Magnolia Bay, Miss Claudia." Nick kissed her on the cheek. "Thank you for inviting us tonight. I always thought your home was a mansion. Now I know it is just that. . .a beautiful mansion that many will get to enjoy over the years."

"Thank you."

By the end of the evening, everyone there had expressed similar thoughts. Cole felt relieved that his plans had received such positive feedback and was proud of his aunt and Ronni for all they'd done to make Bay Inn so inviting and comfortable. It wasn't until after everyone left that he had a chance to tell them, though, and then they all were busy with the cleanup.

"I think we'll have wonderful word-of-mouth advertising after tonight," Claudia said as she gathered the unused plates and cups to take to the kitchen. "The members of the city council were lavish in their compliments."

"I talked to Nick, and he's already spreading the word through his contacts. You can be sure I'll do the same in Dallas."

Ronni turned from loading the dishwasher and held up a hand. "Whoa! We're booked through Labor Day, now. I don't think it will take long to be booked until Christmas."

"Do you think we'll have guests that time of year?"

"I don't see why not—unless you want to close the inn for a few weeks then. Some do."

"I'm not sure," Claudia said. "I guess that's something we need to discuss. But to tell you the truth, I'm a little tired tonight."

"There's not much left to do, Mom. You go on up. I can finish here," Ronni said.

"Are you sure?"

"She's sure," Cole answered for Ronni. "I'll help with what's left to do."

Claudia yawned. "All right then. I think I'll call it a day. Good night, dear ones. Thank you for tonight."

Cole turned to Ronni when his aunt was out of hearing range. "I hope this all isn't going to be too much for her."

"She'll be all right. I think it's just this last week of getting things ready and all the excitement that's tired her." Ronni put the detergent in both dishwashers—they had two, now—and turned them on.

"I hope so. I am so glad you accepted the position to manage the inn, Ronni. I do think that might have been too much for Aunt Claudia."

"She'll have enough to do just being the hostess. I think she's going to enjoy it, though."

Cole grinned, thinking back to the way his aunt had

flitted from one group to another this evening. "I do, too. I haven't seen her so animated and happy in a long time."

"Me, either. And it did go really well tonight, didn't it?"

"It did. I can't tell you how impressed I am with how you and Aunt Claudia pulled everything together so well."

"Thank you, Cole." Ronni's face flushed pink at his compliment.

"Ronni, I. . .thank you for always being there for Aunt Claudia," Cole said, taking a step toward her.

"She's always there for me, too."

"I know." Cole reached out to touch that irresistible curl that always needed to be tucked behind her ear.

"Congratulations on all the wonderful reviews from the party tonight."

"Thank—"

Cole didn't give her time to finish the sentence before he pulled her in his arms for a hug.

"—you." She sounded a bit breathless.

It was about time he let her know how he felt. If she couldn't return those feeling, well, he'd just have to accept it and go on, but he couldn't keep coming here week after week. . .or move back and live here and continue to hide his feelings. It was just too hard.

He tipped her face up to his, and his lips claimed hers for what was meant to be a quick kiss. . .that turned into something. . .somewhat. . .longer. . .than he'd anticipated. The deep thud of his heart was almost painful inside his chest as Ronni suddenly broke the kiss and ran upstairs.

Cole stood in the empty room. If she didn't realize how he felt now, then it was likely she never would.

sixteen

Ronni barely closed the door to her room before tears flooded her eyes. There was no more denying how she felt about Cole. She was in love with him. Deeply and completely. How had it happened? And why had she let it?

She let herself out onto the balcony off her room and sank down into the wicker chair. Taking deep breaths of the fragrant night air, she tried to will her heart to slow down as she looked out toward the bay. It was a beautiful night, made even more so by the realization that Cole did feel something for her, too.

But that only led to more confusion. She didn't want to be hurt again. Not the way Brian had hurt her. The only way to prevent that pain was not to fall in love again. But she loved Cole, in spite of all her determination not to.

He was kind and considerate; his faith in her ability to run Bay Inn had made her confident in her abilities to do so. He loved Claudia just as she did, loved this old home and wanted it to stay in the family, loved this town and wanted to save it. And he cared about her. She knew him well enough by now to know that he wouldn't have kissed her if he didn't.

And that kiss. . .it had taken all the willpower she had to end it. Being in his arms, sharing that kiss—and they had shared it, for she was well aware that she had responded to him—had felt so very right and more than a little wonderful.

Deep down, Ronni was sure that Cole was nothing like his cousin, that he would be faithful to anyone he loved. But she was more frightened than she'd ever been in her life at the thought that she could be wrong about him. She had certainly been wrong about Brian.

The sound of a door shutting came from below, and Ronni stood up and leaned over the rail. Cole was doing stretches before he started his jog. She'd watched him take off on several nights, wishing she had the courage to call out to him to wait for her. Now, she saw him start up the trail and wished she was with him.

As he rounded a bend in the trail, she looked heavenward for her answers. "Dear Lord, please help me to know what to do. Should I deny my feelings for Cole? Or rely on my instincts that he is a good and honorable man who I can trust? I don't know what to do here, and I'm so afraid of being hurt again. Please help me, Lord, before I let myself in for more heartache. In Jesus' name, I pray, amen."

Ronni went back inside just as a soft knock sounded at her door. With Cole out jogging, it had to be Claudia. She hurried to open the door.

"Mom? Is everything all right?"

"I'm fine, dear. Just too keyed up to sleep. But maybe it's me who should be asking you that question."

Ronni couldn't hide the unshed tears in her eyes, and at Claudia's words, they threatened to spill over.

"I'm all right."

"No, dear. I don't think you are. Let's talk." She proceeded to the love seat in front of the fireplace and patted the empty space beside her. "Come sit."

Ronni did as requested after grabbing a box of tissues from her bedside table. She dabbed at her eyes and tried to convince Claudia she was fine. "I guess I'm just having a little reaction to the evening."

"Did something happen after I came upstairs? Cole didn't say anything to hurt your feelings, did he?"

"Oh no!" *He made me feel cared for and so special.*

"What is it then?"

"I. . .he. . ."

"What? What did he do?"

"He kissed me." There. It was out.

"Ahh." Claudia smiled. Then the smile faded. "You are upset that he did?"

"Yes. . ." That wasn't totally honest. "No. . ." Neither was that. "I don't know."

"I see."

"Mom, I—"

"Ronni, dear." Claudia took one of her hands in her own. "Nothing would make me happier than to see you and Cole fall in love."

"But I. . .am so afraid to. . ."

"To trust that he won't be like Brian?"

The tears spilled over. "I'm sorry, Mom, I—"

"Ronni, *I* am sorry. Sorry that I raised Brian to think only of himself and that he hurt you so badly that you are afraid to let yourself love again."

"Mom, it's not your fault."

"Well, I'm not sure of that, but I do know this much: Cole is nothing like Brian. He is the man I always wished Brian would become. Cole is a wonderful, steadfast Christian. He is honorable and loving, and I think the Lord has plans for the two of you."

Was it possible? Ronni didn't know. But she felt a glimmer of hope at the thought that it might be. "I'm not sure about that, Mom."

"Well, dear, all I can say is that you will have to decide whether to throw away a chance for true happiness with Cole on your own, or to trust the Lord to guide your heart in your answer. Much as I would like to play matchmaker, I learned a long time ago to leave that kind of thing in the Lord's hands. But it is my belief that He brought Cole into our lives. . .similar to His bringing Boaz into Ruth and Naomi's lives."

Ronni's heart seemed to swell within her chest. She loved that story. Could Claudia be right? Or was the spark of hope she felt just wishful thinking?

Claudia hugged her. "I'll be praying that you make the right decision, dear. I love you as my daughter. You will always be that to me. I only want what's best for you."

"I know you do, Mom. You've always been there for me. I love you, too."

"Well, now. Let's both put things in the Lord's hands—truly put them there—and know that He will take care of it all. Sleep well, dear."

๛

Surprisingly, Ronni did sleep well. She didn't know if she was just too emotionally exhausted to mull everything over or not, but after saying her prayers and asking the Lord to help her know what to do, she drifted right off.

She was a little anxious as to how to react to Cole the next morning, but he made that easy by treating her the same as always except that when their eyes met, his gaze seemed to rest on her just a little longer. She wondered if she'd ruined whatever chance they might have had by running upstairs after he kissed her. Yet she still wasn't sure that she had the courage to take the chance that he might really care for her.

She was disappointed to find out that he was leaving that afternoon to go back to Dallas instead of after church the next day.

"Oh, Cole, I was hoping you'd be able to stay all week," Claudia said.

"I was planning to; but I received a call this morning, and there are things I really need to take care of so that I can be here for the grand opening. I'll be back on Friday evening to help with any last-minute details, though."

Ronni wondered if he was leaving because of her. She didn't know and didn't have the courage to ask. She only knew she would miss him terribly.

❧

Ronni stayed busy during the days, and the week passed swiftly with all the last-minute details to see to about the grand opening. There was so much to do, and she and Claudia barely saw each other until dinnertime.

But busy as she was during the day, at night Ronni had plenty of time to think over what Claudia had said to her. Alone in her room, she'd done a lot of soul-searching and was coming to the conclusion that her mother-in-law might be right. Cole was very much like Boaz in the way he saw to her and Claudia's needs—finding a way to help Claudia out of the mess Brian had left her in and giving Ronni the opportunity to feel confident in her abilities to use the degree she'd worked so hard for. He helped them in all kinds of ways and watched over them, caring for them and easing their worries about the future. That he was a good and faithful Christian had become obvious in the past few months. His faith was real, and he lived it, unlike Brian. The two men were as different as night and day.

But what Ronni really came to realize was that it was the Lord who had been the busiest in her life—taking care of her needs and meeting the heartfelt wishes she was afraid to dream about by bringing Cole into her life.

It was very hard to come to the realization that while her love of the Lord and her faith in Him had grown, she hadn't totally understood just how He could work in her life—to heal her hurts and make her strong enough to trust her heart to someone again. But He had. Humbled by finally appreciating His care of her day-to-day life, she went to the Lord in prayer.

"Dear Lord, please forgive me for not trusting that You would take care of me. Thank You for helping me to weather the storm of pain that Brian caused and for bringing me to the other side. Now I pray that I haven't ruined things with Cole by running from him the other night. Please help me make things right with him and give me the courage to let him know how I feel. In Jesus' name, I pray, amen."

As the grand opening neared, it seemed Ronni missed Cole more each day. She kept telling herself that his home was in Texas and hers was in Mississippi—it would be hard to carry on a long-distance relationship. Besides, she told herself, if that kiss meant as much to him as it had to her, he wouldn't have gone back quite so quickly. Then she reminded herself that she was the one who ran out of the room, not Cole. She'd probably run him off.

~

Cole couldn't wait to get back to Magnolia Bay. He hadn't wanted to leave in the first place, but the strain in Ronni's eyes the morning after their kiss told him he had to be patient. She had much on her mind with the grand opening of Bay Inn, and he didn't want to add to the stress of the week. But he was afraid he might have already done that. He should never have taken her in his arms that night; he should have waited until after the grand opening. But she'd felt so right there he just hadn't been able to resist kissing her.

Nor had he been able to quit thinking about it. She had responded to his kiss. That's why it had been so very sweet and why he hadn't been able to end it. He couldn't believe her lips would have clung to his if she didn't care about him. But Ronni had pulled away and had run out of the room, and he just wasn't sure that she would ever give them a chance for happiness after all the hurt she'd suffered.

He figured the best way to give her some space, and him patience, was to be in Dallas. But he had to talk to Ronni on this trip. He had to find out where things stood between them. He'd decided to make Magnolia Bay his home, and he felt he must let her know. If she didn't care about him the way he cared about her, well, he'd have to accept it and go on, but he didn't want to do it in Dallas. This small town had become home to him because it held the two people he loved most.

Cole pulled into the drive, hoping to catch Ronni alone and talk to her, but it didn't take long for him to realize their conversation wasn't going to happen just yet. They'd been invited to dinner with the Chamberses, and there certainly wouldn't be any chance to talk to Ronni alone at the restaurant. She looked quite lovely, though. And she did seem pleased to see him; at least he thought she did.

"Are you all ready for the big day?" he asked her.

"I think so. I certainly hope so." The smile she gave him was so beautiful it tightened his chest. He did love this woman. And he wanted to tell her. Soon.

"It's going to be a wonderful day. Our first guests start arriving at noon, and we should be full by tomorrow afternoon," Claudia said.

Suddenly, it dawned on Cole that, with the inn offering both morning and evening meals, their cozy family dinners wouldn't be happening for a while. He knew he would miss them.

By the next morning, he realized that getting time alone with Ronni that day would be nearly impossible. She seemed to be everywhere all at once. She was checking with the cook on the day's menu as she'd had a call from one of the guests informing them she needed a special diet. Once they came up with a substitution for her, Ronni had to call the florist to find out where the flowers for the reception area were. Eventually, everything fell into place, but Cole could tell it didn't happen as easily as it appeared. Ronni had to keep one step ahead of everyone else.

From the time the first guests arrived until after dinner that night, he couldn't remember seeing Ronni sit down. She seemed more elated than tired when he joined her and his aunt upstairs after saying good night to their guests, and he had a feeling now was the time to try to talk to her.

"You ladies have really put in a day. I got tired just watching you."

"Actually, I feel quite energized. I'm sure that might change once I take a long soak, though," his aunt said.

"I'm a little keyed up, myself," Ronni said. "I think everything went really well today."

"I'd say it did. All the guests seem thrilled with their accommodations, and they loved the food—especially the prime rib with those buttered new potatoes. I also overheard one guest say that she'd never had better desserts anywhere," Cole said. "But I saw behind the scenes, and I know how much work you put into today to make it all go smoothly."

"Thank you," Ronni said. "You going for your jog tonight?"

"I think so." She'd never asked him that before. He didn't have anything to lose by asking. "Want to join me?"

"Yes. I think I do."

Cole's heart hammered in his chest, but he tried to tell himself not to read anything into her acceptance of his invitation. "Good. Let's get our shoes on."

Once they were back in the living room, his aunt gave a big yawn.

"Sure you don't want to go with us, Aunt Claudia?" Cole teased.

"Not likely, dear, but thank you for the invitation. I'll see you two in the morning. I'm going to indulge in that long soak," Claudia said. "Good night."

"Night, Mom," Ronni said.

"Sleep well, Aunt Claudia," Cole added before turning back to Ronni. "Ready?"

"Ready."

Her smile gave him courage. He held out a hand. "Let's go."

She took it, and his heart sang with hope.

⁂

Ronni kept up with him quite well. He'd asked if she wanted to walk instead, but when she said no, he quickly realized that she'd been using the trail when he wasn't around.

They passed several of the inn's guests out for a moonlit walk, but by the time they got to the lookout over the bay, they were alone.

"Let's stop a minute and sit. I don't feel like we've had a chance to talk for way too long," Cole said.

"Okay." Ronni took a seat on the cement bench, and he sat down beside her.

"It's so beautiful here. I can't imagine living anywhere else."

"Neither can I." Cole had his opening. Now was the time. He turned to her. "Ronni, I think I owe you an apology for the other night."

She sat up, her chin lifted just a touch, before he realized she might think he was apologizing for kissing her.

"Not for the kiss."

She seemed to relax but didn't look at him.

"Never for the kiss."

Her gaze finally met his.

"I'm apologizing for not telling you then and there how much I love you."

She opened her mouth to speak, but he put a finger over her lips. "I know you may not be ready to hear it and that you may not return my feelings just yet. . .or ever. But the fact is: I do love you. And I'm moving back to Magnolia Bay. It's always meant home to me. . .even more so now. I want my future to be here. And I want it to be with you—no matter how long it takes to convince you that I'm nothing like Brian. I want to spend the rest of my life trying to show you how much I love you if you'll give me the chance."

He removed his finger from her lips but tipped her face up so that her eyes met his, and he waited for her response.

"It's probably not going to take quite as long as you might think, Cole. I'd kind of like my future to include you, too." Her lips met his in a kiss that convinced him she was ready to put Brian in the past and give her trust to him.

Cole wasted no time. "Ronni, I promise to cherish the woman you are for always. I love you with all that I am. Will you please marry me?"

"Oh, Cole, I love you, too—with all my heart. And yes, I will marry you."

Cole claimed her lips once more, thanking the Lord above for healing Ronni's heart and enabling her to finally be able to love again.

epilogue

Late September

On the unusually crisp day, Ronni put the finishing touches to her makeup and hair before letting Meagan assist her in putting on her wedding veil. She'd dressed in her old room, which was now a guest room, so as to have only one flight of stairs to come down to the strains of the wedding march.

The last few months had been busy and exhilarating with getting Bay Inn running smoothly and hiring and training an assistant to help run it while she was away—for her and Cole's wedding trip and whenever they might decide to make a quick trip.

Cole had opened his firm's offices in one of the empty buildings in downtown Magnolia Bay, and Ronni didn't know who was happier about it: him or her. . .or Claudia.

Claudia would be sitting at a place of honor representing both bride and groom today, and Ronni knew that without her mother-in-law's complete approval, it would have been hard for her and Cole to get to this point.

Meagan secured the short veil to Ronni's hair and fluffed it around her face. "Ronni, I've never seen you look lovelier."

Ronni turned toward the mirror, and she almost didn't recognize herself. She loved the pale yellow veil and silk suit she'd chosen to wear, but it wasn't what she had on that was so amazing to her. It was the flushed face, the glowing eyes, the truly happy woman who hadn't been visible until Cole Bannister came into her life.

Each day she seemed to grow happier, and since their engagement, Ronni had known a joy she'd never before experienced in her life. Cole treated her as if she were the most wonderful woman in the world, and she thanked the Lord daily for helping her to realize what a great man he was. She knew he would be a fantastic husband and that she would cherish his love for the rest of her life.

Meagan looked at her watch. "It's time."

Ronni gave her a quick hug before they left the room. Meagan was her only attendant, and she led the way to the top of the stairs. She motioned to Tori, who signaled that it was time for the wedding march to start. As the strains of the music began, Meagan took the first step, and Ronni followed, her heart beating to the tune of the music.

Friends and family were gathered in the wide foyer and largest living area, but she didn't see them. All she could see was the look in Cole's eyes as she headed straight toward him. He loved her. She could see it in his expression and feel it in his touch as he took her hand when she reached his side.

As they turned and recited their vows to one another, Ronni sent up a silent prayer, thanking the Lord above for giving her a second chance at love and for opening her eyes to understand that He had.

When the minister pronounced them husband and

wife and she and Cole shared their first kiss as a married couple, Ronni knew full well how blessed she was to be able to love again.

A Letter To Our Readers

Dear Reader:
In order that we might better contribute to your reading enjoyment, we would appreciate your taking a few minutes to respond to the following questions. We welcome your comments and read each form and letter we receive. When completed, please return to the following:

Fiction Editor
Heartsong Presents
PO Box 719
Uhrichsville, Ohio 44683

1. Did you enjoy reading *To Love Again* by Janet Lee Barton?
   ❏ Very much! I would like to see more books by this author!
   ❏ Moderately. I would have enjoyed it more if

   _____

   _____

   _____

2. Are you a member of **Heartsong Presents**? ❏ Yes ❏ No
   If no, where did you purchase this book? _____

   _____

3. How would you rate, on a scale from 1 (poor) to 5 (superior),
   the cover design? _____

4. On a scale from 1 (poor) to 10 (superior), please rate the
   following elements.

   ____ Heroine   ____ Plot
   ____ Hero   ____ Inspirational theme
   ____ Setting   ____ Secondary characters

5. These characters were special because? _____

   _____

   _____

6. How has this book inspired your life? _____

   _____

   _____

7. What settings would you like to see covered in future
   Heartsong Presents books? _____

   _____

   _____

8. What are some inspirational themes you would like to see
   treated in future books? _____

   _____

   _____

9. Would you be interested in reading other **Heartsong
   Presents** titles? ❑ Yes ❑ No

10. Please check your age range:
    ❑ Under 18   ❑ 18-24
    ❑ 25-34   ❑ 35-45
    ❑ 46-55   ❑ Over 55

Name _____

Occupation _____

Address _____

City, State, Zip _____

Hearts♥ng

Presents

HEARTSONG
P R E S E N T S

If you love Christian romance…

$10.99

You'll love Heartsong Presents'
inspiring and faith-filled romances by
today's very best Christian authors. . .DiAnn
Mills, Wanda E. Brunstetter, and Yvonne Lehman, to
mention a few!

When you join Heartsong Presents, you'll enjoy four
brand-new, mass market, 176-page books—two contemporary
and two historical—that will build you up in your faith when
you discover God's role in every relationship you read about!

Mass Market 176 Pages

Imagine. . .four new romances every
four weeks—with men and women like you
who long to meet the one God has chosen as
the love of their lives…all for the low price
of $10.99 postpaid.

To join, simply visit www.heartsong
presents.com or complete the coupon
below and mail it to the address provided.

✂ -

YES! Sign me up for Heartso♥ng!

NEW MEMBERSHIPS WILL BE SHIPPED IMMEDIATELY!
Send no money now. We'll bill you only $10.99
postpaid with your first shipment of four books. Or for
faster action, call 1-740-922-7280.

NAME_____

ADDRESS_____

CITY_____ STATE _____ ZIP _____

MAIL TO: HEARTSONG PRESENTS, P.O. Box 721, Uhrichsville, Ohio 44683
or sign up at **WWW.HEARTSONGPRESENTS.COM**